THE REVELATION IS LOVE

BARBARA CARTLAND

.com

Barbaracartland.com Ltd

THE BARBARA CARTLAND PINK COLLECTION

Barbara Cartland was the most prolific bestselling author in the history of the world. She was frequently in the Guinness Book of Records for writing more books in a year than any other living author. In fact her most amazing literary feat was when her publishers asked for more Barbara Cartland romances, she doubled her output from 10 books a year to over 20 books a year, when she was 77.

She went on writing continuously at this rate for 20 years and wrote her last book at the age of 97, thus completing 400 books between the ages of 77 and 97.

Her publishers finally could not keep up with this phenomenal output, so at her death she left 160 unpublished manuscripts, something again that no other author has ever achieved.

Now the exciting news is that these 160 original unpublished Barbara Cartland books are already being published and by Barbaracartland.com exclusively on the internet, as the international web is the best possible way of reaching so many Barbara Cartland readers around the world.

The 160 books are published monthly and will be numbered in sequence.

The series is called the Pink Collection as a tribute to Barbara Cartland whose favourite colour was pink and it became very much her trademark over the years.

The Barbara Cartland Pink Collection is published only on the internet. Log on to www.barbaracartland.com to find out how you can purchase the books monthly as they are published, and take out a subscription that will ensure that all subsequent editions are delivered to you by mail order to your home.

NEW

Barbaracartland.com is proud to announce the publication of ten new Audio Books for the first time as CDs. They are favourite Barbara Cartland stories read by well-known actors and actresses and each story extends to 4 or 5 CDs. The Audio Books are as follows:

The Patient Bridegroom	The Passion and the Flower
A Challenge of Hearts	Little White Doves of Love
A Train to Love	The Prince and the Pekinese
The Unbroken Dream	A King in Love
The Cruel Count	A Sign of Love

More Audio Books will be published in the future and the above titles can be purchased by logging on to the website www.barbaracartland.com or please write to the address below.

If you do not have access to a computer, you can write for information about the Barbara Cartland Pink Collection and the Barbara Cartland Audio Books to the following address:

Barbara Cartland.com Ltd., Camfield Place,
Hatfield, Hertfordshire AL9 6JE, United Kingdom.

Telephone: +44 (0)1707 642629
Fax: +44 (0)1707 663041

THE LATE DAME BARBARA CARTLAND

Barbara Cartland who sadly died in May 2000 at the age of nearly 99 was the world's most famous romantic novelist who wrote 723 books in her lifetime with worldwide sales of over 1 billion copies and her books were translated into 36 different languages.

As well as romantic novels, she wrote historical biographies, 6 autobiographies, theatrical plays, books of advice on life, love, vitamins and cookery. She also found time to be a political speaker and television and radio personality.

She wrote her first book at the age of 21 and this was called *Jigsaw*. It became an immediate bestseller and sold 100,000 copies in hardback and was translated into 6 different languages. She wrote continuously throughout her life, writing bestsellers for an astonishing 76 years. Her books have always been immensely popular in the United States, where in 1976 her current books were at numbers 1 & 2 in the B. Dalton bestsellers list, a feat never achieved before or since by any author.

Barbara Cartland became a legend in her own lifetime and will be best remembered for her wonderful romantic novels, so loved by her millions of readers throughout the world.

Her books will always be treasured for their moral message, her pure and innocent heroines, her good looking and dashing heroes and above all her belief that the power of love is more important than anything else in everyone's life.

"The moment you know you are in love – and you will always know instinctively – you are closer to Heaven than at any other time in your life."

Barbara Cartland

CHAPTER ONE
1897

The foaming sea was as wild as an untamed horse and the decks of the transatlantic liner travelling towards England were empty – except for one hardy passenger.

Rupert Fitzalan was caught up in the excitement of the turbulent sky, the power of the waves and the tossing of the ship.

No bucking bronco could be any more unsettling, he felt, remembering the time he had tried for success at a rodeo in the Mid-West of America. He had stayed on the animal longer than most, including himself, had expected, but had been thrown in the end.

Now he stood with spray lashing at him and found the exhilaration of the storm matched his own.

Rupert Fitzalan was going home to Scotland!

The last time he had been home was twenty-three years ago when he was eight years old.

His father, Malcolm Fitzalan, had quarrelled with his proud and irascible parent, Lord Fitzalan, and his two elder brothers had already fallen out with the Laird and left Scotland.

Now the last son took his wife and son and sailed to America. Soon after their arrival, Rupert's beloved mother succumbed to typhoid and his grieving father then devoted himself to building up a successful railway empire.

The deck door behind Rupert opened and a Steward caught him by the arm.

"My Lord, we cannot allow any passengers outside on deck when the sea is this rough."

It was still a novelty to be addressed as, 'my Lord'.

In the years since Rupert's family had left Scotland, both his uncles had died abroad, one in a sinking ship, the other in a riding accident. Neither had left sons.

Two years ago his father had suffered a fatal stroke and Rupert was left in sole control of the railway company.

Last month had come the news that Lord Fitzalan, Rupert's grandfather, had died and the title and estates had come down to his last male descendant.

Rupert was now Lord Fitzalan.

He smiled at the Steward and came inside.

"Can I provide your Lordship with a brandy?"

"Why not?"

Rupert went through to the empty Saloon and chose a seat commanding a fine view of the huge waves.

As he waited for his drink, Rupert conjured up his memories of the ancestral home of the Fitzalans.

To eight year old Rupert, Castle Fitzalan had held out all the drama and atmosphere of its bloody history. He remembered his grandfather recounting tales of feuds with other Clans and dastardly attacks his doughty ancestors had repelled.

Rupert's father had scoffed at these tales.

"That's all in the past. Our future is in America!"

So it had proved.

Many a time, though, Rupert had recalled the erect figure of his grandfather, so full of pride and belligerence and wished he could see him again.

His father had often suggested to Lord Fitzalan that they visited, only to be repulsed.

Now Rupert was returning to Scotland and whether or not he would leave America permanently was a decision he was happy to leave for another day.

Just as he had left the question of marriage.

One of the most eligible young bachelors in New York, he had earned the nickname, *Rupert the Rock*, for it was said that no girl had managed to break his heart.

He had squired some of the loveliest girls around, most of whom had made it clear they would be delighted to become his wife. He had been bored by even the most intelligent of them.

His father had been upset.

"We need to consider the Fitzalan inheritance," he had counselled his son just before he died.

"Plenty of time yet, Father."

"Just what is it you are looking for, son?"

"I want to be as much in love with the girl I marry as you were with my mother."

"I was blessed, but I can see plenty of girls who are beautiful and have sufficient character and intelligence for you to fall in love with."

"None of them moves me, Father, and none of them has that special something – and please don't ask me to define what that is, because I only know I will recognise it when I see it."

With that his father had to be content.

Would he, he now wondered, find a Scottish girl who could command his heart the way his beautiful mother had commanded his father's?

He savoured the fine cognac brought to him by the Steward and dismissed all thoughts of marriage.

It was enough that soon he would have fulfilled his long-held dream of returning to his ancestral home.

It was sad that his grandfather would not be there and even sadder that his father was not inheriting, but even these regrets could not prevent the excitement building up at the thought that soon he would see Castle Fitzalan again.

*

A few days later, Rupert hired a horse in Pitlochry, the Highland town he had reached by rail, having arranged for his luggage to follow him and armed with directions to Castle Fitzalan, he set out on his way.

Little white clouds scudded swiftly across a bright May sky. Fresh lime-green young leaves were on the trees, golden stars of celandine peeked out through grass verges.

Then the land grew starker as the road rose higher and higher becoming little more than a dirt track.

For some time now there had been no hint of any habitation and Rupert began to wonder if he had lost his way. He took out his compass and, not for the first time, checked his direction.

Then, suddenly right ahead he saw rock rising sheer above the track with above it, Castle Fitzalan.

'Nearly there,' Rupert thought joyfully as his horse blew through his nose and shook his head, as much as to say, 'you can't expect me to climb up that sheer face'!

They followed the path as it climbed steeply round the rocky outcrop until it reached heavy studded oak doors set in impenetrable stone walls.

Rupert dismounted and hammered on the doors.

Nothing happened.

He hammered again hard and wondered if the letter announcing his arrival had gone astray. True, he had not been able to state any definite date and time, but surely the Castle staff must be aware he could turn up at any time?

A small window high up in the Castle was thrown open and the barrel of what looked remarkably like an old-fashioned blunderbuss poked out.

"If ye'll not stop yer yammering, I'll let ye have it in the face – so help me if I don't!"

Rupert stepped back and, grasping his horse's reins with one hand, held up the other in a gesture of surrender.

"I'm no enemy. I am Rupert, Lord Fitzalan."

After a moment a face replaced the blunderbuss in the window.

"It'll no be that young Malcolm's boy? Wait ye off there awhile."

The face disappeared and the window closed.

Rupert waited as his horse cropped grass at the side of the pathway.

Soon there came the sound of a heavy lock being opened, then, slowly but smoothly, one of the great doors was drawn back and Rupert entered into his inheritance.

No sooner was he and his horse inside than the door was pushed shut again by a stooped figure with bandy legs wearing an aged kilt.

The doors secured, the figure turned and grabbed one of Rupert's hands. Watery eyes that had once been a bright blue looked hard into his face.

Then the wrinkled face broke into a broad smile.

"If it isn't Master Rupert come back to us! Man, but you're a real sight for sore eyes. I thought ye'd never get here."

Rupert searched his youthful memory for his name.

"It's Duncan, ye ken? I used to ride with ye when ye were nobbut a lad."

With a shock he recalled his grandfather's favourite servant who accompanied him everywhere.

Twenty-two years ago Duncan was upstanding at six feet with a fine head of dark hair. Now not only had he shrunk into this stooped figure but his hair was wispy thin and yellow-white.

Rupert returned the grasp of the hands that held his.

"Duncan, of course, I remember you. Did you not receive the letter I sent announcing my arrival?"

Duncan gave a cackle of laughter.

"The postie doesna get up here. I go out and collect what there is from the village store when I can, but it's not often I get awa'. It's only me and the lad now, ye ken?"

"The lad?"

"That be me, sir. Walt, sir," came a small voice at his elbow. "Will ye no let me take yer horse, sir?"

Walt was a half-starved looking youngster with a huge thatch of dirty straw-coloured hair and an even more raggedy kilt than Duncan's.

"He'll need a good rub-down and water and oats as he's carried me from Pitlochry and it's a longish journey."

"Pitlochry, a fair mile indeed," said Duncan. "And I think you could do with a dram and some nourishment ye'self. Come awa' in."

Duncan led the way over a courtyard where weeds were growing between flagstones.

Everywhere were signs of neglect.

The stone façades needed repointing, the windows were filthy and several were broken. What had once been a lawn now had chickens scratching over it.

"I'm sorry I could not be here for the funeral," he remarked, following Duncan into the Castle.

"Aye, it'd have done yer heart good to see the many folk who came to honour the Laird. Sit ye down there."

Rupert let his aching limbs down into an armchair.

Weekly hacks in Central Park were obviously not enough to keep him in condition for the sort of ride he had undertaken that day.

They were in the kitchen with a small fire burning in the grate.

Duncan slapped a horn mug on the table and poured amber liquid into it from a leather bottle.

"Get yersel' outside that, Master Rupert."

"Duncan, it's good to see you again," said Rupert, sampling the surprisingly good whisky.

Though why was it a surprise? He remembered his father first introducing him to the delights of single malt.

"It's a blessing to have ye here," Duncan exclaimed fervently, helping himself to a large swig from the bottle.

"Why were you threatening me with that ancient firearm?" asked Rupert curiously.

"Ach, it would be those devils – the MacLeans!"

"The MacLeans?"

"The Laird and young Hamish, his son."

"Why should they call?"

Clutching his whisky, Duncan sat down in the other chair.

"The Laird told me that there was some matter of a treasure, an heirloom the MacLean claimed was his. When he first came round here demandin' it, the Laird sent him off like a wee fieldmouse from a fierce cat. No one could put terror into a soul like the Laird."

Rupert thought about the tall towering figure of his grandfather and of the times he had seen him in a rage over some transgression or other. He could well understand his power over other men.

"After that while the Laird was still alive, MacLean kept his distance. The instant the Laird died, MacLean was hammering at the door again."

Duncan quaffed more whisky.

"He'll no rest until that treasure is his – "

"What is this heirloom?"

Duncan shook his head.

"I dinna ken. Any more than did the Laird. Twas enough for him that MacLean should'na have it."

Rupert rose, ignoring his stiffening muscles.

"Can you give me a tour of the Castle, Duncan?"

The old man jumped up immediately.

"Ay, that I can, Master Rupert."

As the tour progressed, Rupert became more and more depressed. The air of dilapidation in the courtyard of Castle Fitzalan continued throughout the building.

There was little furniture or items of value, curtains were in shreds, dust and cobwebs everywhere.

On the walls were portraits so blackened with age it was almost impossible to make out whether they were male or female.

Except for one.

Rupert stopped in front of a full-length portrait in the main reception room.

"I remember this one. It's my grandmother, isn't it, Duncan?"

"Aye, it is. That's the Lady Stella all right."

"As a young boy, I didn't realise quite how lovely she was."

Lady Fitzalan stood tall and straight with one hand on the head of a wolfhound, abundant dark hair drawn on to the top of her head. Dark eyes laughed at the viewer and a generous mouth curved deliciously.

She wore a green gown with a tartan scarf arranged diagonally across her breast and fastened over one shoulder with a large cairngorm brooch.

"Aye, she was that lovely," agreed Duncan, staring at the portrait.

Then he gave himself a shake.

"Well, you'll be wantin' to see the rest no doubt – "

By the end of the tour Rupert recognised that there was a huge task ahead of him to bring Castle Fitzalan back to its former greatness.

For food that evening, Duncan produced a venison stew. It had been a long time since Rupert had been served such simple fare, but not only had his journey given him a hearty appetite, the dish tasted delicious.

They ate in the kitchen for Rupert had no wish to suggest he be given his meal alone in the huge and echoing dining room.

After finishing his meal, he sat back feeling deeply satisfied.

"Duncan, my thanks. You're a splendid cook. You also seem to have handled everything at the Castle since my grandfather's death – and probably before that as well – with great efficiency."

He paused, looking to reassure the old retainer.

"My father and I built a very successful business in America and now I can afford to staff and restore the place, bring it back to its old glory."

Duncan rose and removed the remains of the stew.

"I'll just be taking this out to the lad," he muttered.

Rupert waited for him to return and wondered if he should have put things differently.

Once back Duncan placed the bottle of whisky on the table and sat down.

"Aye, Master Rupert, this place needs a might of money spent on it. The fabric's sound enough, but I doubt it'll be that easy to find staff, but I can see ye need to try."

"I hope you will remain in charge, Duncan," Rupert suggested and the ancient retainer seemed reassured that he was not going to be pensioned off.

"I'll go back to Pitlochry tomorrow,' he continued. "There's a man there looking out a decent horse for me and I can see I will need one."

He needed to ride every day. The horsemanship skills while he lived in California, building up the railroad company, were very rusty. His move back to New York on his father's death meant he walked or travelled in carriages and cabs.

"Aye," muttered Duncan, poker-faced.

When Rupert asked Duncan about Castle Fitzalan's neighbours, he shrugged off any idea of social life.

"The Laird wouldn'a have had dealings with any of those MacLeans or the others around here – 'a mean, close lot' was what he called them."

Gradually Rupert came to the realisation that his grandfather had done little with the last fifteen or so years of his life.

"I do wish my father and I had come back to visit before this," he stated at last.

Duncan gave him a slightly bleary look.

"And the Laird wished that too. He didn'a say it, but as his three sons, one by one, fell by the wayside, I knew he felt it."

Rupert felt deeply ashamed.

He and his father should have just turned up, not waited for an invitation.

Duncan refilled the mugs.

"Right auld sod the Laird could be," he mumbled, then rose and picked up the blunderbuss from where it had been resting beside the window.

"I'll be awa' to ma bed, now, Master Rupert, and you'll be wantin' yours, too, I reckon. Ye've no need to concern yersel with safety, I'll be sleeping with this!"

Rupert made his way to the room that Duncan had earlier indicated was where he would be sleeping.

The large four-poster bed had been well supplied with fresh linen and a heavy coverlet. A series of prods indicated a horsehair mattress in reasonable condition.

He placed the jug of hot water he had brought for his ablutions on a rickety table and took his weary limbs to bed.

*

Rupert occupied the long ride back to Pitlochry the next morning planning how he could restore the Castle. It would, he decided, be an enjoyable experience.

He had been impressed with the Castle's situation on the banks of a lake that he must learn to call a 'loch', and the wild beauty of the surrounding countryside.

Despite Duncan's words Rupert was sure there had to be possibilities for a social life and that the MacLeans, whoever they might be, would prove at the very least to be interesting or even hospitable.

A life building up the railroad business had taught him never to judge a person by background or reputation. Once you were able to talk directly to them, it was possible to find something stimulating about almost everyone.

Having inspected the horses that had been found for his consideration, Rupert finally settled on a stallion with a coat that was almost all white with a proud head, combined grace with strength and justified his name, 'Prince'.

"Excellent choice, my Lord," said the Agent. "He's a wee bit on the pricey side, but worth every penny."

Rupert managed to bring the asking price down a little and reckoned that the deal was not a bad one.

Having returned his hired horse, Rupert presented himself at the offices of James Cunningham, the lawyer who had been handling all the legal matters surrounding his grandfather's death.

"Lord Fitzalan, it's a pleasure to meet you." Mr. Cunningham came forward to shake Rupert's hand.

Solid walnut furniture and bookshelves full of legal volumes supported the view Rupert had already made from their correspondence that this was a man well able to cope with his affairs.

Once all the necessary papers had been signed and decisions taken on necessary legal questions, Rupert raised the matter of Castle Fitzalan and its condition.

Mr. Cunningham shook his head.

"It's been a real tragedy, my Lord. Lord Fitzalan's income over the last ten years or so came almost entirely from selling off anything of value. There's been nothing coming in from the land, you understand? And against all my advice your grandfather made some bad investments."

The lawyer tapped his fingers on the wooden desk in a gesture of frustration.

"If only he had asked my father," said Rupert sadly.

"Too proud for all that. And your uncles who died abroad within a few months of each other left debts he felt in duty bound to honour."

"My father did write to my grandfather at the time suggesting he came over, but all he received back was a curt message not to bother."

Mr. Cunningham sighed.

"There's no feud pursued with such endless passion as a Highland feud and Lord Fitzalan held that all three of his sons had betrayed him."

Rupert sat in silence for a little, thinking about his grandfather's difficult life. Then he enquired,

"Speaking about Highland feuds, Mr. Cunningham, what can you tell me about the MacLeans? According to Duncan, my grandfather's retainer, they have been trying to gain entry into Castle Fitzalan. Some sort of story of a stolen heirloom."

"Ah!"

Mr. Cunningham straightened his papers.

"I know nothing about any heirloom. Given Lord Fitzalan's parlous financial state, any such treasure would almost certainly have been sold. However, there is a story that Lord MacLean felt that your grandfather had stolen the affections of the woman he intended to be his wife."

"Would that be my grandmother, Stella?"

"I believe so. It all happened a very long time ago and who is to know the truth? However, there has been bad blood between the MacLeans and the Fitzalans for as long as I have known them."

"You know the MacLeans?"

"My Lord, it's a small world here in the Highlands. The MacLean estate borders the Fitzalan's. I believe there was a time the two clans were friendly – but they are no more."

He shot a keen glance at Rupert and added,

"I would listen carefully to your retainer and watch your step. Lord MacLean is as stubborn and proud as your grandfather was and has a reputation for ruthlessness that is matched only by that of his son, Hamish."

*

Rupert rode back to Castle Fitzalan enjoying the strength and liveliness of Prince.

He tried to dismiss the details of the MacLeans.

He had experienced enough business feuds to know the lengths that men could go to when money and power were at stake.

But his grandfather had had neither.

And there was no sign at all of an heirloom in that rundown Castle.

The portrait of his grandmother?

Rupert considered this possibility for no more than a moment before dismissing it. The head of the MacLeans was hardly likely to risk his life for the portrait of a woman who had refused him.

Perhaps, he contemplated as dusk deepened and he neared the end of his journey, he could suggest a meeting to Lord MacLean to try and sort the matter out?

Now in the failing light of day the empty beauty of the moors acquired a sinister aura.

Strange shapes seemed to loom in front of him and he longed to reach the Castle and to know that Duncan was watching out for him.

Suddenly straight out of the gloom, came a posse of horsemen, shrieking and wielding staves.

They fell upon Rupert and dragged him off Prince.

His head received a massive blow and he knew no more.

CHAPTER TWO

The red squirrel leapt from tree to tree.

As it settled on a branch, Celina Stirling, her bright hair as red as the squirrel's, raised her shotgun and took careful aim.

She took in its frothy tail, its delicate paws and its enquiring face and then lowered the gun for just a moment before bringing it up again and pulling the trigger.

The animal swiftly leapt from its branch to one on a neighbouring tree.

Celina looked up with satisfaction at the centre of a large knot on the tree, now riddled with her shot.

There, that would prove it to Hamish MacLean her accuracy with a gun, and there was no need to slaughter a poor squirrel.

Unconsciously she glanced again at the citrine ring on her engagement finger.

Two weeks ago now Hamish had asked her to be his wife.

She picked up the empty game bag and set off back towards Beaumarche Castle, remembering the visit she had paid this morning to her mother's old friend, Lady Bruce.

"Celina, my dearest girl, do you really intend to go through with this match?" Lady Bruce had asked bluntly once she was sitting by a blazing fire in her salon.

Though the sun was shining, it was dark and chilly inside Beaumarche Castle, the MacLean ancestral home.

Over the past two weeks Celina had fantasised over how she would transform this old place once she became Lady MacLean.

Nothing could be changed whilst her uncle, Lord MacLean, was still alive and it looked as though he would survive a great many more years yet.

"What sort of a question is that, Aunt Margaret?"

"You are cousins, my dear. It has never seemed to me a suitable union."

Celina tossed back her flowing hair.

"It is one that seems very suitable to me."

She poured coffee and handed a cup to Lady Bruce.

"Thank you, my dear. I do so wish that when your dear mother and father died in that dreadful accident, you could have come to me. At twelve years old to be brought up in an all-male household did not seem at all right. I did try to persuade your uncle, but alas without success."

The light in Celina's eyes softened for a moment.

"You have kept a close eye on me and the MacLean household, Aunt Margaret," she replied lovingly. "I have always known I could come to you if I was worried about anything."

Lady Bruce smiled at her.

"Your mother was my closest friend and nothing would have given me more pleasure than to have the care and upbringing of her daughter.

"You are in a rather delicate position, Celina. You are a very lovely girl and heiress to a sizeable fortune when your Trust fund matures on your thirtieth birthday."

Celina rose abruptly and stalked around the room.

"Hamish and I have always been the best of friends. I have never met a more exciting man. He is always doing something most unexpected. There are so many activities we both enjoy and he has taught me to shoot and fish and we love riding together and I am proud to be a member of the MacLean family."

"Oh, how like your mother you are," Lady Bruce exclaimed. "When she met your father she could not wait to be wed and they were so very happy together. Then you came along and life seemed perfect to them. You must be as proud to be a Stirling as you are a MacLean."

Celina came and knelt before her.

"I am indeed, dear Aunt Margaret. I apologise for my outburst. It is just that anyone suggesting Hamish and I are not a perfect couple makes me upset."

She looked pleadingly into Lady Bruce's eyes.

"My dear," her Godmother placed her hand on her shoulder, "I did not mean to upset you and I hope that you will both be very happy. Now, where are Hamish and Lord MacLean?"

"They are out – "

Lady Bruce had hit upon a sore point. Hamish had promised to take her fishing that morning, but instead, after breakfast he had told her to go and practise her shooting.

When she had asked to go with him, he had told her off for answering him back and instructed her to bring him back a squirrel.

Celina had taken a deep breath, prepared to tell him he should not speak to her like that, but Lord MacLean had shouted at Hamish to come at once.

She had watched them leave, the harnesses of their horses jingling as they rode off together with several of the MacLean retainers, for all the world as though they were back in the sixteenth century and about to take on a party of English warriors.

"Out?" queried Lady Bruce.

Celina said nothing.

"The news is all over the area this morning that the new Lord Fitzalan has arrived from America," she added conversationally. "I hope that your uncle has no thought of maintaining that stupid vendetta he had with the old Laird. Apparently Castle Fitzalan has been quite stripped of all its valuables. It's a bare inheritance that young man has come into."

"I just don't care, Aunt Margaret, the Fitzalans are a bad lot – they have harried and cheated the MacLeans since time immemorial. I expect that the new Laird will be every bit as bad as the old."

"My dear!"

Lady Bruce looked scandalised.

"There are no grounds for carrying on this feud."

Because Celina was so fond of her Godmother, she turned the conversation into other areas.

It was mid-afternoon by the time Celina was able to take out her shotgun to provide proof of what an excellent marksman she had become.

Remembering Lady Bruce's reservations about her engagement, Celina could not help also recalling Hamish's curt rejoinder to her when she had dared to tell him she did not need to practise her shooting.

It had indeed been a stupid thing to say – shooting always needed practice, but his tone and the supercilious way he had looked at her had been quite unacceptable.

She would have to make it clear that *she*, Celina Stirling, would not stand for such behaviour.

Smiling to herself, as she was sure that Hamish had merely been in a hurry and did not want to upset his always impatient and autocratic father, Celina returned her weapon to the Beaumarche gun room.

As she placed it in the rack with the other shotguns, she glanced across the room to where the handguns were kept.

To her dismay, she saw that several were missing.

Why should Hamish and his father need to go out armed? With alarm she remembered the news Lady Bruce had brought – that young Lord Fitzalan had arrived.

Surely they had not gone out to confront him and demand return of the heirloom?

Tales of the late Lord Fitzalan's exploits tumbled into Celina's mind.

According to her uncle, he had always been willing to take a shot at the MacLeans. The heir was American, no doubt used to fighting Indians in the Wild West!

Along with his title and the Castle, he would surely have inherited the feuding obsession of the Fitzalans and would almost certainly emulate his grandfather's habit of using gunfire to get his way.

Celina sat in the Great Hall waiting for her fiancé and uncle to return.

*

As darkness began to fall, she grew more and more apprehensive.

What had happened?

Was Hamish lying dead outside Castle Fitzalan?

And her uncle?

There had been half a dozen or so riders who set out that morning, surely there had to be at least one person left alive to return and tell what had happened?

She thought of tall Hamish with his mane of blond hair and riveting blue eyes and choked back a sob.

Fire smouldered in the huge grate. A log slipped its position, sent up a shower of sparks, then leaped into life.

Shadows flickered in the vast and ancient Hall.

Though the major part of Beaumarche Castle had been built in the eighteenth century, the Great Hall with its tattered MacLean standards belonged to medieval times.

Even with the roaring fire, it was cold in the chilly May evening. Celina pulled her plaid wrap more securely round her shoulders.

The Steward entered.

"Will you be a-waitin' for his Lordship and Master Hamish to return before supping, Miss Celina?"

Celina nodded, unable to trust herself to speak.

"They'll have come across game, I'll be thinkin'. Out of season, but that'll no be stoppin' his Lordship."

Celina took a deep breath.

"I am sure you're right, Robertson," she murmured, trying to believe it herself.

The Steward added two massive logs to the fire.

Then, suddenly, the Great Hall was full of men.

There was Lord MacLean striding in, his face alight with satisfaction, surrounded by five hard men, their faces grimly pleased, slapping each other on the back.

And there was Hamish!

Celina started towards him, her heart singing with relief, then stopped as she realised that it was not a dead stag he carried over his shoulder – *but a man*.

As she stopped, stunned, he threw his burden to the ground.

The man cried out in pain as he landed, his eyelids fluttered and then opened.

Celina saw that his hands were bound and that he had suffered a severe blow to the back of his head and his dark hair was matted with blood.

"Gained consciousness, have you?" Lord MacLean snarled at him.

Celina ran to Hamish and slipped her hand through his arm.

"What has happened?" she whispered. "You were away for so long, I was frightened something dreadful had happened."

His eyes sparkling, he put his hand on the back of her neck and looked down at her.

"*That* – " he pointed to the half-conscious body on the floor, "is the new Lord Fitzalan.

"Completely in our power," he added, purring as if he could imagine nothing more satisfactory.

Celina gasped and stepped back.

The wounded man stirred, then levered himself into a sitting position and looked about him with heavy deep-set eyes and Celina saw that they were a dark grey flecked with silver.

As they caught sight of her, something flashed in their depths.

Then with athletic agility, hands still bound behind his back, he somehow managed to stand upright.

"I regret you should have had to see me in such an ignominious position," he mumbled to Celina.

Lord Fitzalan was tall, much taller than Hamish.

He lacked Hamish's brawn, but his rangy wiriness suggested an equal strength.

He had a strong-boned and authoritative face.

"Why have I been set upon in this way?" he asked, speaking slowly in a firm voice that betrayed a faint hint of an American drawl.

Celina felt an odd shiver go down her spine.

Lord MacLean struck him across the face.

"You'll not speak until you're spoken to, boy."

Celina gasped again and brought her hand to her mouth, unable to believe what was happening.

Lord Fitzalan's lip curled.

"That afraid of me, are you?"

He appeared to be in command of himself now.

"You are a cur," sneered Lord MacLean.

"That does not explain why you have brought me here," his prisoner stated steadily, looking the older man straight in the eye.

Despite her deep hatred for everything the Fitzalans stood for, Celina could not help admiring the way this one conducted himself.

"We should clean his wound," she suggested in a low voice to Hamish. "I'll fetch some water and a cloth."

He grabbed her wrist painfully hard.

"You will do no such thing," he barked. "This man deserves nothing."

"You have something *special* that belongs to us," Lord MacLean flared up. "It is time it was returned."

"Something that belongs to you? What would that be?" Rupert asked, his voice calmly questioning.

"You know, damn you."

Lord MacLean struck him again across the face.

Rupert briefly closed his eyes as his head jerked to the side and then opened them to stare again at his captor.

"It's our MacLean heirloom, damned Yank," yelled Hamish, dropping Celina's wrist and standing beside his father. "Don't tell me you don't know what it is."

Celina gently massaged her wrist where Hamish's cruel grip had caused painful bruising.

She felt bewildered as she had never seen this side of her fiancé before.

"*An heirloom*?" Rupert repeated slowly. "I know nothing about it."

"Your grandfather did," Lord MacLean exclaimed, leaning in towards him and almost spitting in his face.

"That man was the lowest of low creatures – he did not deserve to crawl upon the earth. He cheated and stole his way through life battening on those whose boots he was not fit to lick. He deprived me and my family of what was rightfully ours *and now we want it back*."

Rupert face set in rigid lines and Celina could see his shoulders tighten.

"And how do you plan to achieve that?" he asked in a voice so cold it sent a shiver of apprehension through her.

This was not a man to be trifled with.

She wondered if Hamish and her uncle understood the nature of the man who stood before them.

"You will take us back to Castle Fitzalan, open its gates and make us free of the place," said Lord MacLean, a giant sneer on his face.

"Even if I did know what you were talking about, I would do no such thing, MacLean. I would not allow any member of your family or any servant of yours to so much as step on the threshold of Castle Fitzalan. My grandfather was a most honourable man and I will not hear his name besmirched in such a disgraceful fashion."

Celina could not help admiring the way this man, his hands bound and his head badly wounded, facing half a dozen powerful and armed enemies, could bear himself so calmly and coldly.

Hamish flushed red.

"How dare you talk to us MacLeans like that! It's our heirloom that the Fitzalans have stolen. We demand it back."

"And what exactly is this heirloom? When do you claim it was stolen?"

Hardly had Rupert stopped speaking than Hamish punched him viciously in the stomach and then gave him an uppercut that forced his head back dramatically.

Rupert fell to the floor and Hamish kicked him, his riding boots giving a sickening blow to his ribs.

Celina cried out and tried to stop him. Before she could reach him, Lord MacLean dragged Hamish back.

"Enough, son. You'll get nowhere this way."

Hamish stood breathing heavily, giving the fallen man a look Celina could not recognise. It seemed to be full of hate.

"Throw him in the dungeon," yelled Lord MacLean to his retainers. "He must learn that it is useless to deny a Highlander his rights."

Several men picked up the unconscious figure and bore him out.

Hamish drew a deep breath and turned to Celina.

"You see what we have to deal with?" he grizzled and held out a hand towards her.

She retreated, her heart so full of horror she thought it would break.

"*How could you*?" she shouted at him.

"Celina?"

She pushed him away, fled from the Great Hall and rushed upstairs to her bedroom. There she flung herself on the bed in a storm of tears.

She had seen the man she thought she loved behave in the most despicable manner.

Celina despised the Fitzalans – but to kidnap a man, to knock him out, then bind his hands behind his back and hit him like that – she could hardly believe her eyes.

*

It came time for the evening meal.

The very thought of sitting and eating with Hamish and her uncle sickened Celina.

She had to know, however, just what they intended to do with their prisoner.

At one end of the Great Hall was a gallery. It was said that in medieval times minstrels would play there for the diners below. Access originally had been via a spiral staircase from the floor of the Great Hall. However, when the eighteenth century extension was built, a long corridor running past the bedrooms gave access from the first floor.

Celina certainly did not approve of eavesdropping, but her need to find out exactly what her uncle and Hamish were going to do was now so strong, she quietly let herself into the gallery and stood in a corner hidden from below.

Lord MacLean sat at the head of the long refectory table with Hamish on his right.

As Celina entered the gallery he was saying testily,

"Where is the girl?"

"Let her be, sir. I care not if she joins us or remains sulking in her room," answered Hamish.

Celina swallowed hard.

"Have a care, son! Your fiancée brings a welcome fortune – and is one of the loveliest wenches around. You need to keep her sweet until her thirtieth birthday. God, if only she had control of her money today!"

"She is mine, sir. I have no doubt of that."

The Steward entered and asked if he should send to see if Mistress Stirling was to dine with his Lordship.

Lord MacLean gave a dismissive wave of his hand.

"She is indisposed. Start the service, Steward!"

The Steward respectfully bowed and disappeared behind a carved screen at the other end of the Great Hall.

Celina then observed Hamish grab a large decanter of red wine and fill both his and his father's glasses, drink down half and recharge his glass.

"That's the way!" cried Lord MacLean.

"So, what is to be the plan for that maverick Yank down in the dungeon?" asked Hamish. "Will you allow me to finish him off after dinner?"

Lord MacLean shook his head.

"Let him sit on cold stone for a night without bread or water. By morning he will be willing to give us the keys to Castle Fitzalan and I will at last gain my revenge on the old Laird."

Hamish poured more wine, then waved the empty decanter at the Steward as he entered with bowls of soup.

"Bring us more bottles," he ordered.

Celina melted away from her corner and returned to her room.

There she sat and ruminated feverishly.

There was little doubt in her mind as to what her future should now be.

More pressing, however, was what should be done about poor Lord Fitzalan.

An hour later she returned to the hidden corner of the gallery.

Lord MacLean and Hamish had finished their meal and the table had been cleared.

The Steward entered with more bottles of wine. As Celina had expected, both were much the worse for drink.

They were greatly enjoying themselves, toasting their achievement in capturing Lord Fitzalan and drinking to the day when their revenge would be complete.

Celina had seen enough.

After a final visit to her room, she walked quietly downstairs and let herself out of the Castle.

As she expected, the stables were quiet. The horses had been fed and watered and the grooms were elsewhere.

She could at once see Lord Fitzalan's stallion as he was the only grey in the stables and he stood out like snow on a dark moor.

And there, hanging in the tack room, were a brand new saddle and bridle.

Working swiftly, Celina quickly made friends with the horse and harnessed him. Hoping no one would come along to stop her, she led him out of the stable.

The stallion followed her obediently as she hurried through the yard to the back drive and finally she tethered him out of sight of the Castle.

Returning, she came in by the back entrance.

Sounds of clearing up and bawdy exchanges came from the kitchen. Moving silently past them, she reached the start of the carved screen that divided the Great Hall from the service passage.

There a flight of stone steps led down to the cellars.

A lantern hung halfway down, throwing a dim light that enabled Celina to hurry down the steps without fear of falling.

She had prepared a story should there be a guard on duty outside the Castle dungeon. She would tell him that Lord MacLean had sent her with a message that he was to join the men in the kitchen and drink to the day's success.

But there was no need as there was no guard.

After all, Lord Fitzalan was safely locked up in the ancient dungeon.

In a niche at the bottom of the stairs were stored a number of candles together with matches, all ready for any servant coming to the cellars.

Celina felt for a candle.

Her hand trembled slightly as she lit it and then she chided herself. This was no time to feel nervous. She took a deep breath, held up the light and walked steadily along the damp stony passage towards the dungeon.

She sighed with relief as she saw that the large iron key to the heavy door hung from its usual hook at the side of the small cell.

With difficulty Celina forced it to turn in the lock.

The door creaked as she drew it open and holding the candle high, she entered.

Rupert stood with his back against the stone wall.

In the flickering light his face looked ghastly but he was fully conscious.

His jacket was badly ripped and his breeches were splattered with mud and she was thankful to see no fresh blood had come from his head wound.

"More blows, is it?" he grunted, "or am I supposed to be so taken with your charms that I will do all you ask?"

His voice was weaker but steady and again Celina admired his courage.

Without speaking she poured a little hot wax onto a stone shelf and stood the candle upright.

"Turn around, please" she asked, forcing herself to speak without emotion.

"So that you can stab me in the back?" came the sardonic retort as his gaze caught sight of the glint of steel she held.

"So I can release your hands – "

Rupert raised his eyebrow and for a moment she thought he would refuse.

"Quickly, I don't know how much time we have," she urged him.

At that he turned and lifted his hands to her knife.

The rope was very thick and the knots too tight to be untied.

Swiftly, she sawed through them, grateful for her foresight in keeping her hunting knife sharp and soon the ends fell apart.

Celina drew in a quick breath as she saw how red and raw both his wrists were.

He swung round to face her.

"Who are you?" he asked, looking at her curiously as he massaged his wrists. "And why are you doing this?"

"I am Celina Stirling, Lord MacLean is my uncle. I have no love for the Fitzalans. I believe your family to be as wicked as my uncle claims, but my honour as both a MacLean and a Stirling will not allow you to be treated as you have been today. Come with me."

She prised the candle off its shelf.

"You are setting me free?"

Rupert remained without moving.

"What else do you think I am doing?" she hissed, exasperated by his slow reactions. "Follow me now. Any moment my uncle may decide to check on his prisoner."

She waited in the doorway, holding her light high, tapping a foot in nervous frustration.

"Can I trust you?"

His light drawl sounded almost amused.

"For Heaven's sake – come!"

Celina hurried off without checking to see if he was following, but almost immediately she heard the quiet click of his riding boots.

She led the way, not up to the kitchen, but along the corridor in the other direction.

The air grew colder and damper.

Behind her she could hear his breathing grow more laboured as she recalled the punishment he had sustained and slowed her pace a little.

He said nothing, but she could imagine how, with his failing strength, he was forcing himself to keep close behind her.

The necessity to spirit him away before her act of disloyalty was discovered combined with her belief that this was a man who would let nothing daunt him, kept her going.

At last the passage began to rise again until there was no room to stand.

"I'm sorry, we need to crawl now," she cautioned.

"Why does that not surprise me?" the ironic voice came from behind her.

She ignored him, taking to her knees and fighting off the claustrophobia that caught her by the throat.

Eventually she reached the grille that closed off the passage. There was no lock on it – it was carefully hidden behind a small fall of water and looked like a drain filter.

Moments later she was through and could stand erect. Then she bent and helped him slide through.

"Phew!" he sighed, managing to stand unsteadily. "For a moment I thought I was back in a Californian silver mine.

"We are getting wet," he added unnecessarily as the spray from the fall gently penetrated their clothes.

"Follow me, my Lord."

A rough path led down a hill to the bottom where the ground was level and easily traversed.

There she turned and surveyed Rupert.

"I am so sorry I had to put you through all that, but there was no other way."

He looked thoroughly exhausted and hardly able to hold himself upright.

"I am happy to be as far away from this place as possible, Miss Stirling."

"Good. Your horse is nearby – "

"Is there no end to all your resourcefulness, Miss Stirling?"

The ironic note in his voice was just beginning to irritate her.

"Follow me, please, my Lord."

"Of course – what else?"

He was stumbling now. They were out of sight of the Castle and Celina slowed her pace.

She turned and saw through the moonlight that he was almost at the end of his strength.

She took hold of one of his arms and put it round her shoulders, saying, "lean on me."

She felt his instinctive recoil and his reluctance to accept her help, then the realisation that he needed to.

As they both staggered along, she could hear how laboured his breathing was and the way it pained him.

Something inside her, despite her strong opinion of the Fitzalans, responded to his condition.

"I hope your ribs are not broken?" she enquired.

"It will not be your cousin's fault if they are not," he managed to blurt out.

At last they reached the end of the back drive.

"Here is your horse."

He removed his arm from her shoulders and almost fell forward onto the animal.

"*Prince.* I thought never to see you again!"

Celina untethered Prince, put the reins into Rupert's hands and helped him to mount.

"Can you manage?" she asked.

He looked down at her.

"Point me in the right direction for Castle Fitzalan and I will do the rest."

She looked up at the bright sky now full of stars.

"You are blessed with a clear night. Look, there is the Plough. See where its handle points? Follow that and you will reach Castle Fitzalan."

"The Big Dipper I know it as," he said. "But how about you? What will happen with the MacLeans?"

"Fear not for me, I can take care of myself, but you will need to watch out if you stay in Scotland. Your escape will not put my uncle and cousin off their crazy mission – they will try to abduct you again."

"Next time I will be ready for them – "

He reached down for her hand.

"You have my most heartfelt thanks, Miss Stirling. I know no man would have done for me what you have."

He raised her hand and brought it to his lips.

"I have not forgotten how you despise my family, but if you ever have need of me at any time in the future, you only have to ask."

He gave her a glimmer of a smile.

"You know where to find me!"

His gallantry moved Celina.

Had it been Hamish in his position, he would not have tarried, but dug his heels into his horse and galloped away without taking his leave.

She slapped Prince's rump.

The startled animal set off, his rider almost falling before managing to raise an arm in farewell.

Celina wrapped her arms round herself and started to walk back to the house.

*

Lord MacLean and Hamish were still at the table, drunk, but not quite incapable as Celina came into the Hall.

She had changed into her riding habit and a cloak.

Hidden beneath it was the revolver she had helped herself to from the gun room.

They looked at her owlishly.

Celina removed the large citrine ring that Hamish had placed upon her finger and laid it on the table.

"*I cannot marry you,*" she stated calmly.

"The devil you can't!" he slurred. "What nonsense is this?"

"I thought you were an honourable man. You are certainly not and I will not join my life to one with so few principles."

"You are being foolish, my girl," came in her uncle. "You have had too sheltered a life. Our honour dictates we retrieve our heirloom."

"Not this way," Celina asserted calmly and walked out of the Great Hall and her life with the MacLeans.

CHAPTER THREE

Rupert never knew just how he managed to reach the safety of Castle Fitzalan.

Afterwards he supposed that the advice to allow the stars to guide him, plus the use of the compass still safely tucked into his jacket pocket, had enabled him to travel in a direction that eventually brought him to familiar country.

It was sheer willpower that kept him in the saddle.

It was still not midnight when he pulled up a tired Prince before the studded gates of Castle Fitzalan.

Duncan had already gone to bed.

"I'd thought ye'd decided to stay in Pitlochry," he cried when at last Rupert's battering on the gate brought him down to open it.

Then he saw the state his new Master was in and was horrified.

"Man, ye need more than a wee drop of the hard stuff. What the hell's been happenin' to ye and ye'll need that wound seeing to, I'm thinkin'. Come awa' in and tell your tale."

By this time Walt had appeared and took Prince off to the stables.

Duncan just managed to catch his Master as Rupert sagged to the ground.

"I'm sorry," Rupert murmured weakly. "I seem to have lost my strength."

Leaning heavily on Duncan, he reached the kitchen.

There he was sat down and was well supplied with whisky before the old retainer riddled the stove and heated water to clean his head wound.

Rupert sat gratefully and watched Duncan at work.

The fiery heat of the alcohol warmed his cold and badly battered body and little by little the vile headache the powerful blow had given him released its hold.

As Duncan cleaned the wound, Rupert told him the story of his kidnapping and how he had been set free by Celina Stirling.

Duncan shook his shaggy head in wonder.

"Mistress Stirling was it who rescued you? Laddie, that's a queer thing – with her affianced to young Hamish MacLean."

Disappointment shot through Rupert.

All the way to Castle Fitzalan he had been filled by a sense of warmth as he remembered the beautiful girl who had freed him.

She had been the first person he had set eyes on as he regained consciousness.

Dressed in a russet gown, blazing red hair flowing down her back, her eyes an astonishingly clear green, she enshrined an almost medieval splendour that enabled him to divorce his mind from what was happening to him.

Too soon, however, he had been forced to summon up all his strength not to collapse under first the verbal and then the physical attack by the MacLeans.

When she had suddenly appeared in his prison cell, illuminated by a flickering candle, he had thought that he was hallucinating.

The fact that she was solid flesh and had come to rescue him was hard to accept, but by the time he had been reunited with Prince and realised the nightmare was over, her clear voice and control over the situation had made as deep an impression on him as her appearance.

Thus the information that she was engaged to the vicious Hamish MacLean came as a deep shock.

Had all that talk about honour been no more than a cloak to cover her real intentions? But what could they be?

Once again his head throbbed unbearably.

"She's a bonnie lass – "

Duncan refilled both their whisky mugs.

"I ken her father – he was a Stirling – her mother was Lord MacLean's little sister. Francis Stirling was a braw lad that courted young Elaine many a moon afore she accepted him. There was a great weddin'."

He lapsed into silence, no doubt remembering the celebrations.

"Of course, the Laird was no invited, but the young couple set up home not so far away. I seen them often out and about, until the dreadful day some ten or eleven years ago they were killed in a train crash. The wee lass went to live with her uncle at Beaumarche Castle."

"So you haven't seen her since she was a child?"

Rupert found he was intensely interested in Celina Stirling's background.

"Aye I have. She's often visitin' Lady Bruce, her Godmother, who was friendly with the Laird. Not that she ever came here, but we would go over there and the young Mistress Stirling was often stayin' with her Ladyship.

"She would never meet the Laird. He said that the MacLeans had poisoned her mind against him with false tales. But I would see her walkin' the grounds whilst the Laird was inside with Lady Bruce and once we talked."

He paused for a moment, considering, then added,

"That was only a couple of years ago and I thought how bonnie she was and how well she comported hersel."

He looked straight at Rupert.

"When I heard that she and yon Hamish MacLean were affiancied, I says to meself that mebbe she would keep him straight. From what I hear he's a fine lad most of the time, but there's that vicious MacLean streak in him that comes out every now and then."

Rupert felt his sore ribs and once again wondered about the motives of Celina Stirling in setting him free.

"Now, I'm thinkin' it's a dish of pottage you'll be needin', laddie, afore you find your bed."

Duncan's meat soup proved to be both sustaining and comforting.

That, combined with the whisky, enabled Rupert to fall asleep almost as soon as he drew the coverlet over his bruised body.

His last thought before he closed his eyes was the memory of Celina Stirling saying that the MacLeans would try to abduct him again. If that was so, then he needed to polish his riding skills.

It had been far too easy for them to take him on that evening and he was *not* going to run back to New York.

*

Over the next several days Rupert divided his time between assessing how Castle Fitzalan was to be restored to its former glory and riding Prince.

Gradually the bruises faded from his body and he determined that the MacLeans would not take him again.

Never far from his mind was the vision of Celina Stirling as she had stood in the Hall of Beaumarche Castle and then appeared miraculously in his cell.

Besides her beauty, there was a certain feistiness about her that appealed to Rupert.

Could he, though, trust her motives in freeing him?

Had it really been the matter of honour as she had claimed?

Her uncle and cousin certainly had no honour.

He had no doubts about his new mount. Prince was proving to be everything he had hoped – strong, fearless, athletic and very fast.

Riding him over the moors soon had Rupert feeling he was well on the way to regaining all his riding skills.

"Laddie, you're a-lookin' twice the man you were when you arrived," Duncan sighed a week after Rupert had returned from his abduction.

Rupert laughed – he found his retainer's easy way of speaking to him surprisingly attractive.

"I've some way to go yet, Duncan. Now, how are we getting on with finding some staff to help you here?"

Duncan waved a dismissive hand.

"Och, weel, there's a strange lack of folk willin' to join us in this draughty auld place."

"It won't always be draughty. Soon, I am going to set a whole programme of repairs and renovation in hand. I have written to a firm of architects that Mr. Cunningham put me in touch with and they're sending a partner out next month to see exactly what is required."

"Have ye now!"

Duncan did not seem as pleased as he had expected. Then he realised that the old man did not want to change his ways too much. For him and his memories of life with his grandfather, the Castle was perfect the way it was.

He went to saddle Prince, wondering how he was

going to bring Duncan round to accepting that life at Castle Fitzalan was going to have to change radically.

It was an invigorating day with a strong West wind blowing and he soon left the Castle behind and set Prince at a gallop.

As the days had passed by without incident, Rupert had gradually begun to feel safe.

After riding at full gallop towards a wooded hill, he slowed to a canter.

Suddenly two men rode out of the trees and, even at a distance, he recognised Hamish MacLean – it was as if the man had burned himself into his consciousness.

Rupert had no wish to engage in a fight today.

So he swung Prince round, only to find another two riders coming up behind him.

He made a quick assessment of the lie of the land.

He was in a valley with two woods on his right and a steep hill on his left. In front the valley passed through two hills along a small river. He remembered that it then widened out. If he could reach it before Hamish and his companions, he should be able to lose them.

He spurred on – then saw that two more men were coming through the gap in the hills.

Once more he was at the mercy of the MacLeans!

This time Rupert would not allow them to take him.

Determination roared through his veins.

He turned Prince towards the steep hill on his left, bent low over his neck and urged him to gallop as he had never galloped before.

The gallant animal responded at once, charging up the rough slope as though it was a grass-lined Racecourse.

It was a bumpy ride and Rupert thanked his stars for

all his riding over the last few days. It had built up his muscles and created a partnership with him and Prince.

Behind him he could hear many loud curses as the MacLeans found their mounts unable to climb up the steep scree-ridden slope with any real speed.

With increasing confidence Rupert urged Prince on.

Then came the crack of a rifle and a bullet grazed his arm.

He continued and behind him heard a shout from Lord MacLean telling Hamish not to shoot as they wanted the fellow captured – not dead.

Well, he thought, smiling grimly to himself, they were not going to capture him that day.

He reached the top of the hill to find that the other side sloped much more gently down.

In the distance was Castle Fitzalan.

"Come on Prince!" he shouted. "There'll be double rations for you tonight."

As though he understood, the horse galloped as fast as if he had not just completed a punishing climb at top speed and Rupert left his pursuers far behind.

*

"Ye've bin that lucky, laddie," mused Duncan after Rupert safely arrived home. "I shall come out with ye next time and I'll be armed."

"We both will be if my grandfather owned anything other than that antique blunderbuss!"

"Before I forgets, Lady Bruce called and left her card."

"Lady Bruce?"

"Ye remember I said she was a near neighbour of yourn? And that the Laird would visit Drumlanrigg from time to time? And it's where I last saw Mistress Stirling."

An unexpected and vivid image of Celina swirled before Rupert's eyes.

"I must return Lady Bruce's call, Duncan. When would be the best time?"

"If ye'll be a-readin' the back of her card, ye'll see she suggests tomorrow for lunch if ye've nothing on."

*

The next day early Rupert set out with Duncan for Drumlanrigg.

Duncan had insisted that he be driven in the Laird's ancient open carriage.

"Then ye can wear yer smart American clothes," he said to Rupert with what could only be described as a leer.

Rupert's main luggage had arrived two days earlier brought by cart over the moors.

He selected a tweed three-piece suit that an English tailor in New York had produced for him.

Across his chest he arranged his father's gold watch on its heavy chain, slipping it into the little fob pocket after checking that it was fully wound up.

It was the only time-piece in the Castle.

Rupert could remember a long-case clock standing in the main hall in his childhood. The face had had a sun and moon that moved with the time. He supposed that the clock had been sold and mourned its disappearance.

He found the carriage waiting for him. Two sturdy but by no means young horses were harnessed to it.

Rupert felt that this whole charade was ridiculous – he would much rather ride over to Lady Bruce. However, he allowed Duncan to hand him in.

It took more than three quarters of an hour to reach Drumlanrigg through towering hills and wooded valleys.

Rupert admired the scenery, but spent most of the journey wondering what Lady Bruce was going to be able to tell him about Celina Stirling and the MacLean's feud with the Fitzalans.

It still felt rather strange to be announced as 'Lord Fitzalan,' but he walked into Lady Bruce's drawing room as though it was the boardroom of his New York Railway Company.

"Lord Fitzalan, I am so pleased to meet you," said his hostess, coming forward. "I was a great friend of your grandfather, though I regret I saw little of him over the last few years as he became something of a recluse."

Lady Bruce was a no-nonsense figure in a tweed skirt and jacket with a pair of *pince-nez* dangling down the front of her silk shirt. Iron-grey hair was arranged in two plaits that circled each ear. Her voice managed to combine authority with a musicality that made it attractive.

Her complexion seemed soft and prettily coloured. Perhaps it was, as his mother had claimed, that the mist and rain of the Scottish climate preserved the skin.

Rupert bowed over her hand as faint memories of a much earlier encounter came to him.

"Were you not at Castle Fitzalan for an archery contest when I was a small boy, Lady Bruce?"

She gave him a delightful smile.

"Fancy you remembering! There must have been a dozen of us there."

"But you won, did you not?"

He smiled back at her, all at once feeling at home in this light-filled room lined with paintings and furnished in chintz-covered chairs and sofas.

Lady Bruce laughed.

"Yes, and I was proud to do so. For your mother ran me a close finish."

She looked at him with genuine sympathy.

"I was so sorry to hear of her death, I did not know her well but I liked her style. And your father and I spent some very pleasant times hunting together."

Rupert nodded, unexpectedly touched.

He had not expected to find anyone who had known his parents, and he could not help speculating what Lady Bruce's relationship with the MacLeans might be and how soon he could bring up the name of Celina Stirling.

"Now, please sit down, Lord Fitzalan."

She waved a hand at an armchair.

"I think you have met my goddaughter – "

A twinkle lit her pale blue eyes as a figure that had been standing unnoticed in the corner of the room behind Rupert came forward.

Celina Stirling was not smiling.

Dressed in a similar style to Lady Bruce in heathery tweed that complemented her red hair drawn back with a brown bow, she looked just as though she would rather be anywhere than here.

Rupert stretched out his hand and then withdrew it as she immediately placed her hands behind her back.

"Celina!" barked her Godmother. "Don't make me ashamed of you."

The girl flushed, the colour highlighting her fine bone structure.

Rupert realised that this was the first time he had had the opportunity to see her in daylight.

The first magical impression he had formed of her was instantly confirmed.

"I am afraid you must think me a desperate rascal," he began, trying to hold the gaze of those huge green eyes with his. "Why you felt you had to rescue me, I cannot imagine, but I don't think I will ever be able to show you how grateful I am."

A stubborn look came over Celina's face.

"I told you, it was a matter of honour – "

"Please – " urged Rupert, wondering how he was to get through to her. "Will you not sit and tell me why the Fitzalans have incurred such enmity from your family?"

She gave him another stubborn look.

"You warned me that your uncle and cousin would make another attempt to kidnap me and I have to tell you that yesterday they did."

At that her eyes flashed.

"But they did not succeed?"

"You see me standing here before you."

"It is more than I expected – "

She spoke with reluctant admiration and came to sit in a chair on the other side of the room.

"I do hope you will tell Celina and me exactly what happened," Lady Bruce commented encouragingly. "The MacLeans are old friends of mine and their actions distress me more than I can say."

She laid a sympathetic hand on Celina's.

"You acted with great courage, my dear."

"She did indeed," concurred Rupert.

Then in his best matter-of-fact manner, he briefly told them of the ambush he had escaped the previous day.

Celina's gaze never left him as he spoke.

Her figure was rigid and the fingers of one hand beat a silent rhythm on the arm of her chair.

Everything about her spoke of her distaste for the gory details, but whether it was because of her relations' conduct or his, he found it was impossible to determine.

"You say you were shot at?" Lady Bruce reacted in horror when he reached that point in his tale. "You were not, I hope, hit?"

"A flesh wound, nothing more. I rather think it was because they could see I was getting away – it was a last desperate attempt to bring me down. Thanks to Prince, my splendid horse, they could not catch me after that."

Celina closed her eyes.

Lady Bruce patted her hand.

"We must be grateful to have Lord Fitzalan sitting with us, hale and hearty."

"What I do not understand," questioned Rupert, "is why the MacLeans are that intent on kidnapping me. Do they really think that they can force me to give them this heirloom they are so desperate to possess? And what is the heirloom? I know nothing about it."

Lady Bruce looked towards Celina, but the girl said nothing, so she gave a deep sigh and answered,

"Lord Fitzalan, the MacLean feud with your family dates back for hundreds of years. Lord MacLean and your grandfather were in love with the same girl.

"Stella was very beautiful and at first she seemed to favour Lord MacLean. They were both seventeen, full of passion and spirit and the engagement was announced.

"Suddenly, however, it was broken off and Stella was to marry your grandfather instead.

"He was ten years older than Robbie MacLean and he looked much as you do now, but I don't think looks had anything at all to do with it. I do suspect it was a matter of personality and no one knows exactly what happened, but since then there was a deep enmity between the two men."

"I think I can understand and if I was engaged to a beautiful girl I was passionately in love with and suddenly an older man then whipped her away from me, I would feel desperate!"

Rupert looked at Celina and knew that he spoke no more than the truth.

A terrible pain filled his heart.

He had never met a girl who moved him the way she did, but he had also never met a girl who looked at him with such hate and despair in her eyes.

"Lord Fitzalan stole my uncle's bride away from him," Celina added fiercely. "He wooed her with promises of a better life and with worldly possessions."

Lady Bruce shook her head.

"The MacLeans have always had more money than the Fitzalans."

Celina seemed to struggle with herself.

"My uncle did suffer reversals in his fortune some years ago. I believe he needs extra funds that will enable him to mend matters."

"Well then, tell him to look elsewhere than Castle Fitzalan," Rupert burst out before he could contain himself.

Celina raised her eyes and shot him an angry look.

He cursed himself for his too-quick tongue – then wondered again why she should have freed him when the MacLeans had him in their power.

Lady Bruce held up her hand.

"Let's not quarrel. Celina, have you any idea what this heirloom is that Lord MacLean is so certain has been stolen from his family?"

Celina shook her head.

"I know nothing of it, Aunt Margaret. Uncle Robert

has called it a treasure brought back from the Crusades and says that he is certain it is in Castle Fitzalan and that it was stolen from the MacLeans way back by a jealous Laird."

Lady Bruce studied her for a moment.

"I assume that it is because the state of his finances worsened that Lord MacLean only recently seems to have been asking for this heirloom's return?"

"He has done more than ask, Lady Bruce," chipped in Rupert grimly. "Duncan, my grandfather's retainer, says that several times he and my grandfather were threatened by MacLean Clansmen turning up at Castle Fitzalan and demanding entrance. Only the use of a blunderbuss sent them away!"

"And you complain that you were shot at!" Celina threw the words at him.

"In both cases, it was the MacLeans who were the aggressors," Rupert shot back.

Lady Bruce sighed.

"You two are both as bad as children, arguing about something you know nothing about. Lord Fitzalan, are you certain that you don't know of anything at your Castle that could be identified as this heirloom?"

Rupert shook his head, wondering if this was the real reason Lady Bruce had invited him to visit her.

Was she attempting to obtain whatever it was Lord MacLean was so keen to claim so that Celina could return it to her uncle and cousin?

"I am sorry, Lady Bruce. Duncan has given me a complete tour of the Castle and it seems to contain little of value. My grandfather appears to have been forced to sell many valuables so he could continue living there."

"So the heirloom has probably gone with the rest," Celina turned on him again accusingly.

Once again he remembered her close relationship with the MacLean Clan and that Duncan had said she was engaged to Hamish MacLean.

Was it really possible that, because of the way they had treated him, she had rejected her relations?

She was not wearing an engagement ring – did that mean she was not going to marry Hamish after all?

Celina Stirling seemed honest and straightforward, but he had known men in his business dealings who turned out not to be as they had initially appeared.

Was it possible that this girl was still working with the MacLeans, hoping to get below his guard?

He tried to ignore this thought and to consider the possibility that his grandfather had sold the treasure.

"I think it unlikely," he replied finally. "He kept the portrait of his wife, Stella, and several pieces that Duncan has said were all Fitzalan Clan heirlooms. My grandfather apparently wanted to conserve an essence of the family to hand on to me."

"There you are!" Celina exclaimed triumphantly. "You've called them 'heirlooms'. How can you be so sure one of them isn't what my uncle is referring to?"

Rupert sighed.

"Do you really think that a carved chest, a Jacobean table or several swords could qualify as this treasure? I do not think any could possibly have been brought back from the Crusades, apart that is from the swords."

"Does any have a jewelled hilt?"

He shook his head.

"They are rusty and look ordinary."

Lady Bruce intervened.

"How complete a tour were you given?"

Rupert turned to face her.

"May I ask, Lady Bruce, what your part inquisition?"

She threw up her hands.

"Good Heavens, I see I have managed to g. t. quite the wrong impression. My dear boy, I hope y. not mind my calling you that – you bring back so happy memories of my old friendship with your fathe grandfather. It is just that this wretched feud is causir. much trouble. Celina has abandoned her family – "

Celina made a fierce gesture and seemed about protest, then subsided as though she had, after all, to adn that it was what she had actually done.

Was she not a good actress or was she tormented by whatever decision she had made?

If so, what was that decision?

"Your grandfather had his last months of life made a misery by this MacLean vendetta and you, Lord Fitzalan, have twice been attacked with the aim of abducting you. The first time you were brutally treated and if it had not been for Celina here, I would dread to think what might have happened."

"I shall be grateful to Miss Stirling until my dying day," he responded simply, wishing that he could dispel his suspicions about her motives for rescuing him.

Once again Celina flushed as Lady Bruce went on,

"Until this shameful question of the heirloom and the truth of its ownership is solved, I can only see matters getting even worse and who knows how they will finish. If there is anything at all I can do to prevent grief and tragedy consuming two families I have long been friends with, then I will do it."

She finished speaking on a resolute note, looking Rupert straight in the eye.

He made a graceful gesture and rose.

"Lady Bruce, I accept all you say, it seems the only way I can be left in peace to restore my ancestral home is to resolve the matter of this heirloom. I thank you for your invitation to luncheon, but I shall go back to the Castle and make a rigorous search. I will then, if you will permit me, return and give you the result."

Lady Bruce smiled.

"Bravo! I do applaud you, Lord Fitzalan. I am sure this is exactly what should be done!"

Celina rose in a single fluid movement.

"I shall accompany you, Lord Fitzalan, as two will be able to search more quickly than one."

He looked at her standing straight and determined before him.

Could he trust her?

If he refused to allow her to accompany him, she would not trust him.

And he could scarcely deny that the prospect of her company was very attractive.

Rupert bowed.

"It will be my pleasure to have your company, Miss Stirling. Lady Bruce, can a message be sent to Duncan to harness up the carriage?"

As they waited, he looked at Celina and wondered again just why she wished to accompany him.

Much as he would like to think that she wanted to find the heirloom so as to end the feud, he was afraid that, instead, she was planning to snatch it from him.

CHAPTER FOUR

As Celina ran up the stairs to collect her wrap, she was filled with conflicting emotions.

Why had she said she must go with Lord Fitzalan to his Castle?

After the terrible scenes at Beaumarche Castle, she had never wanted to see him again.

The man was a member of the hated Fitzalan Clan and, worse than that, he had revealed sides of her uncle and cousin that were truly horrifying.

This meant she had to leave Beaumarche. Now any reminder that her relations could behave in such a barbaric way was more than she could bear.

When Lady Bruce had told her in the morning that she hoped Lord Fitzalan would take luncheon with them, she had wanted to scream.

"I just cannot meet him again, Aunt Margaret," she shuddered. "He is a *monster*."

"Of course he's not. Lord Fitzalan is not going to beat or abuse you in any way. If what you have told me is true and I am quite certain it is in every respect, he will be enormously grateful to you."

"I don't want his gratitude. Please, Aunt Margaret, don't make me meet him. I will keep to my room until he has left."

"Nonsense, girl. You will behave like the Lady you are and greet him politely."

Because she so loved her Godmother and respected her judgement, Celina had composed herself, calming the blood that raced around her veins.

She tried to tell herself that Lord Fitzalan was only an ordinary man who had been caught up in extraordinary circumstances, but she had placed herself so that when he entered the drawing room, he would not be able to see her.

His athletic walk and the confident way he carried his exceptional height took Celina by surprise.

With a sudden stab to her chest, she recalled that at their previous meeting, he had been so badly beaten that he could hardly stand upright.

Then he turned round to face her and she saw how delighted he was at her presence.

Something sublime seemed to happen inside her – it was as though his smile turned her bones to liquid and she had difficulty in preventing herself collapsing into a chair.

She could not understand her reaction.

This was the Fitzalan who had brought disaster on her, who had revealed the vicious side of Hamish and lost her the one man she had thought she loved, her friend from childhood days.

Lord Fitzalan had made it impossible for her to stay any longer in the Castle she had called home for so many years, and she could hardly bring herself to address him in anything approaching a civil manner.

She had seethed inwardly at the way he seemed so relaxed in Lady Bruce's drawing room – this *savage* from the primitive shores of America.

She seethed even more when he would not accept her account of his grandfather's behaviour, or the existence of the precious heirloom the Fitzalans had filched from the MacLeans.

She had wanted to fly at him, beat her fists against his chest, force him to acknowledge the rightness of their claim. Instead she had sat rigidly in her chair, determined she would force him to open up Castle Fitzalan.

And then he had confounded her by declaring that he would scour the place for the heirloom.

Immediately she knew that she had to be at his side when he searched.

Otherwise he could easily bury it somewhere on his vast estate and declare he had found nothing. It was what her uncle and Hamish had feared his grandfather would do.

No – much as she hated the idea of having to spend time in close contact with this man, it was essential that she accompany him to Castle Fitzalan.

Celina found her wrap and returned downstairs.

She then said goodbye to Lady Bruce and listened to Lord Fitzalan's assurances that he would return her to Drumlanrigg before dark.

"The Castle is not that large and we will soon have searched every nook and cranny," he smiled.

Lady Bruce stood still thoughtfully at the top of the steps looking worried as she watched them leave.

Celina realised that she felt responsible for the fact that her goddaughter was disappearing without a chaperone in the company of a man she hardly knew.

This did not worry Celina. She was used to living in an almost completely male household and riding around the countryside without a companion of any sort.

"Afternoon, Mistress Stirling," Duncan greeted her, as he descended from the driver's seat of the carriage, his broad grin revealing gaps in his teeth.

Celina remembered that he had once brought the old Laird over to a reception at Lady Bruce's.

She had remained in the garden so that she did not have to meet the old Lord Fitzalan. She had observed him arriving and, despite herself, been impressed by his striking looks.

With flowing white hair, eagle nose, erect posture and muscular legs beneath his kilt, he looked, she thought, like an ancient hero from an ancient folk tale and then she remembered who he was and walked to a different part of the garden so that she need not encounter him.

When later she had seen Duncan in Lady Bruce's garden, curiosity had made her respond to his respectful greeting and spend time talking to him. She had warmed to his admiration of Lady Bruce's roses and found herself agreeing what a pity it was that his Laird's Castle had no formal garden.

Now she nodded to the retainer and said she hoped that he was in good health.

"Aye, that I am, miss."

"Miss Stirling is to visit Castle Fitzalan with me, Duncan. We are to search the place for some heirloom or other."

"So that's the way of it, is it? I mind me the Laird once said somethin' about a missing heirloom."

"He did?" Rupert enquired eagerly as Celina was helped into the carriage. "What did he say about it?"

"Only that it be a shame he couldna put his hands on it as it might prove an answer to all his problems."

Rupert looked so disappointed that Celina felt she had to say,

"You cannot expect Duncan suddenly to produce all the necessary details, my Lord!"

He turned to her with a rueful smile.

"Is it wrong to want to solve this awful situation as quickly as possible?"

"Of course not," she replied as Duncan clicked the horses into action. "I think we all want it found and Lady Bruce and I certainly do, but, forgive me, my Lord, if I say that finding the heirloom is only half of what is needed."

"Ah, I do see what you mean. We need to ascertain without a scintilla of doubt its ownership, isn't that it?"

Celina was grateful for his quick understanding, but feared that he assumed he would be able to prove that the owners were the Fitzalans.

"Suppose," she responded slowly, allowing him to arrange a rug around her knees. "Suppose it can be proved 'without a scintilla of doubt', as you say, that whatever the heirloom may turn out to be, it belongs to the MacLeans, so will you hand it over to them?"

She glanced up at him and found he was looking at her with great seriousness.

Once again her bones felt as if they were turning to liquid.

She swallowed a small gasp of distress, tried hard to remove her gaze from his and found that she could not, as she was drowning in the depths of his silvery-grey eyes.

"Like the surface of a loch under a spring breeze," she murmured as if only to herself.

"I'm sorry, what did you say?"

"Nothing," she stammered, at last taking control of herself.

She tried to remember how much she disliked and distrusted him.

"I was waiting for your response to my question. I think, my Lord, that you imagine just because the heirloom may be in your Castle, that automatically means it belongs to you. I am suggesting that you may well find proof that it does not. What then, will you do? Prove yourself just a bigoted Fitzalan?"

She finished with a contemptuous toss of her head.

He did not move his gaze from hers.

"Oh, dear, Miss Stirling, what a very poor opinion you have of me and my family. Let me assure you that if the heirloom is found and it does indeed prove to belong to the MacLeans, then I shall have great pleasure in handing it straight over to your uncle, if only to prove that I and my family are men of honour."

"You could hardly do anything else if I am present when you find the proof!"

She regretted the words as soon as they left her lips.

She watched how his eyes narrowed, their grey now that of flint, saw the stillness that entered his body, the way his mouth tightened.

"I think we shall ignore that remark," he muttered at last in a cold voice.

She flushed deeply and was at last able to tear her gaze away from his and instead look out at the landscape, but she could not have said what scenery they were driving through.

"Ye'll no be findin' yon cursed heirloom at Castle Fitzalan, I'm thinkin'," said Duncan cheerfully. "The auld Laird knew every inch of the place."

"I think we have had enough talk of this wretched treasure," Rupert's voice was now much more friendly. "I think I should prepare you slightly for what you certainly will find at the Castle."

Her hand on the side of the carriage as it rattled on over the increasingly rough road, Celina listened to a light-hearted account of his arrival at his ancestral home.

"There was I with a picture in my mind of how it had been when my parents and I had left twenty-two years ago when I was eight and you could not have been born."

"I would have been a year old," murmured Celina.

She was twenty-three now.

And it had taken her some time to agree to marry Hamish. Had she, she still wondered, hesitated for so long because she sensed that the high spirits she loved so much in him could turn into something less attractive?

Had she glimpsed something of his dark side in the way he hunted down stags and then gralloched them with unnecessary force, tearing out their vital parts?

She was not sure that Rupert had heard her confess her age, for he continued,

"I do remember our departure with absolute clarity. My grandfather had locked himself in his room and would not come to say goodbye. My mother pressed my father to make one last attempt to talk to him and to try once again to explain why he felt there was no future for our family in Scotland. He went upstairs – but it was no use."

He paused for a moment.

"It was a departure full of emotion. Perhaps that is why I remember exactly how my childhood home looked as we left."

Celina listened intrigued to his story of a medieval Castle little changed from the thirteenth century, but filled with a variety of furnishings gathered over several hundred years of domestic living, giving it a rich and comfortable appearance.

"It was a right bonnie place," intervened Duncan.

"And that was what I expected to find on my return and instead I was greeted by just an empty shell!"

"Not all empty," protested Duncan. "I was there to welcome ye."

"With a blunderbuss!"

"Och, well, that's the MacLeans' fault."

Duncan stopped the carriage on a rise and pointed with his whip.

"There be it, the Castle Fitzalan, Mistress Stirling. Have ye no seen it afore?"

She shook her head.

"Never."

A square battlement was stabbed with slit windows, as its top blossomed into a fairy-tale collection of turrets. The plaster coating of the grey stone was in a poor state of repair – it came away in parts, suggesting that the whole structure was enfolded by giant cobwebs.

Celina was familiar with this very Scottish style of architecture, but she had never seen one as captivating or as mystical as Castle Fitzalan.

As she stared, totally entranced, Duncan flicked the horses' reins and they continued until the carriage finally climbed a steep slope and reached closed gates. There he had to shout at the stable lad to open up before they could enter the sadly neglected courtyard.

Celina could see that Rupert had not exaggerated the state of his home.

In the salon the plaster had completely fallen away from the walls and all was dust and dirt.

She could hardly believe that Castle Fitzalan, the seat of the powerful and supposedly rich Fitzalans could be this rackety and rundown.

The magic of her first sight of the place dissolved into the reality before her now.

Almost as if he could see it all through her eyes, Rupert ventured apologetically,

"I am trying to put an army of women together to perform a spring-clean."

"If there's to be a whole load of work done after your smart architect comes down, there'll be no point in cleanin' now," said Duncan. "It'll only have to be done all over again. I suppose ye'll be wantin' somethin' to eat?"

"A bowl of one of your soups a little later, Duncan, would be great, but I think Miss Stirling and I should start our search right away."

Rupert looked at Celina.

"Should we start at the top or the bottom?"

"The top," suggested Celina briskly.

She was feeling uncomfortable at the closeness of this man and the light in his eyes as he looked at her.

Not even Hamish had stirred such a complex set of emotions in her.

If only he was not a Fitzalan!

"Right then that is where we shall start."

Rupert led the way up a series of spiral staircases.

At the top of the Castle there was a long gallery with a large window at both ends. There were shelves but no furniture – and, apart from dust and the odd book lying on its side, the shelves themselves were empty.

It took no more than a few minutes to ascertain that the walls and ceiling were not hiding a secret cupboard.

Despite herself, as she followed Rupert out of the gallery and then through a succession of small rooms that seemed to cling onto the sides of the Castle, Celina found herself studying her guide.

How thorough and systematic he was in his search.

She was used to the erratic ways of the MacLeans and had not realised how much she had been irritated by their slipshod methods of going about anything, including this matter of the heirloom.

Soon she realised that she and Rupert were working as a team, dividing the rooms to be searched, then meeting again outside each, shaking their heads.

"Do I gather you are trusting me not to overlook a hiding place or stash the treasure away?" he remarked after they had dealt with several rooms in this fashion.

She flushed at the teasing note in his voice as all her suspicions of him flooded back.

"I'll know if you try anything like that," she replied sharply.

He looked exasperated.

"Why do you find it impossible to believe that what I want most in all the world is to find this wretched piece of treasure, whatever it is? I want to bring an end to a feud I have had nothing to do with that is ruining my life."

Then he looked deep into her lovely eyes and his expression softened.

"No, I lie. There is one thing I want more than that – *it is for you to trust me.*"

Celina found her heart beating so fast she thought it might suddenly fly out from her breast.

"Come on then, my Lord" she exclaimed, "we have only searched half of your wretched Castle!"

They descended to the main floor and he held open the door of yet another room for her.

"Yours, I think," he suggested expressionlessly.

She strode past him – into a large salon.

Here two armchairs stood in front of a huge stone fireplace and a wooden door was set into one of the walls.

She opened it and was faced with the dusty shelves of a cupboard on which were three ancient bottles of wine. She picked them up and automatically checked their labels.

"Worth drinking?" asked Rupert.

"I thought they might be Napoleon brandy. I heard Uncle Robert say once that it was very valuable."

"Not in those shaped bottles."

"You've tasted Napoleon brandy?" she asked him, suddenly intrigued.

"I once bid for some in a wine auction, but was out-gunned. A shame – I still wonder what it tastes like."

He picked up one of the bottles.

"Hmm, a very decent claret. Shall we drink it with Duncan's soup?"

Celina shrugged her shoulders.

For the briefest of moments it seemed that they had forgotten both their mission and their suspicions of each other.

Had they met under any other circumstances, she thought sadly, they might well have been friends.

Then as she turned to survey the other side of the room, she was transfixed by the portrait hanging there.

"What a beautiful woman," she cried. "Is she your grandmother, the woman Uncle Robert wanted to marry?"

Rupert nodded, watching her closely as she studied the painting.

"I don't wonder that she had two men desperate for her!"

She felt sad for her uncle.

The woman he had finally married many years after losing the love of his life had died giving birth to Hamish, so Celina had never met her, but she had seen photographs that suggested she had been pretty without much character.

She turned angrily away from the vibrant-looking beauty on the wall.

"I just wonder how your grandfather forced her to renounce my uncle."

"She was'n'a forced," said Duncan, as he entered the room, "it was a real love match right enough. She died when ye were a wee laddie, and the Laird never recovered from her loss. She sent for me before her end and made me promise to stay with him."

Duncan turned away but not before Celina had seen a moistness in his eyes.

"I came to tell ye the soup is ready. Ye'll have to make do with the kitchen, though, Mistress Stirling."

Celina took a last look at the painting.

"I'll not be minding that, Duncan, and I could do with some soup – it's hungry work searching this place."

"Thirsty, too." Rupert held up the bottle, "and I'll bring this with us."

The kitchen was no better than the rest of the house, but the range gave out a welcome warmth and Duncan's vegetable soup was very tasty.

"You're an excellent cook, Duncan," Celina praised him as she tucked into her steaming dish.

Rupert prowled listlessly round opening cupboards and going through to the outer scullery and searching there.

"Ye'll no find what you're lookin' for down here, laddie," remarked Duncan. "All them cupboards are bare.

"I'll go check on the horses," he added and left the kitchen.

Rupert sat down at the kitchen table to his soup.

"I do hope that you don't take offence at Duncan's informality. He's been here for so long he's now one of the family."

"We're all used to straight dealing from servants in Scotland," Celina assured him.

Rupert put down his spoon.

"I have a terrible feeling that we are not going to be successful!" he grimaced.

"But that is what you want, is it not?" Celina could not stop herself saying. "To be able to claim you tried and failed?"

Rupert suddenly thumped on the table with his fist, making the soup slop out of his bowl.

"You are the most infuriating girl I have ever met! Why can't you believe that I do actually *want* to find that dreadful whatever-it-is? Do I look so Machievelian? So untrustworthy?"

Taken aback by the strength of his attack, Celina almost choked on her soup.

"Just look at me!" he insisted. "What do you see? Someone who is determined to deprive a rightful owner of his property?"

Those silver-grey eyes were now full of passion as they regarded her.

Again she felt that melting of her bones and now it seemed as though a bird was beating its wings against her heart, making it impossible for her to breathe.

His expression changed once more and he reached across the table towards her.

Celina leapt up from her chair, stormed over to the window and, her back to him, took several deep breaths.

The thudding of her heart gradually quieted, but she could feel his gaze fixed on her.

Finally she turned round.

"You don't understand, do you? You treat it as a joke. Well, it isn't! If you had lived with the MacLeans, if you had heard them going over and over the wrongs that have been done them, how they hate all Fitzalans and how this heirloom would solve all their difficulties, you would not speak as you do."

He looked grim.

"I think I really do understand, Celina. After all, I have been abducted, beaten and shot at. That does rather concentrate a man's mind, you know? If you had not freed me, I would be in a very sorry state. That is why I have allowed you to enter this Castle. I would not have allowed any of your relations in."

"I know," she muttered simply recalling his bravery facing her uncle and Hamish.

For a moment his eyes narrowed and then he rose.

"Right, we will complete our search and I pray that we shall find whatever cursed object it is that your uncle believes should be his."

Rupert swept out of the room and Celina hurried to follow him.

*

No treasure was found in any of the other rooms.

The last one to be searched was a muniment room, lined with shelves containing deed boxes, documents and leather-bound books.

"Have you looked at these?" Celina asked him.

"In case they contain clues to an heirloom? I made a quick assessment of them when I first arrived. They are mostly account books and estate records."

He started taking down some of the deed boxes and opening them.

"These all contain various legal documents."

Celina looked over her shoulder.

"Suppose that the heirloom is hidden elsewhere, my Lord? Just suppose that after the Fitzalans stole it from the MacLeans, they found a safe place. Wouldn't the Laird of the time make a note of where he had concealed it? And wouldn't he place the details with his legal documents in case he died before telling anyone else where it was?"

He looked at her with amusement.

"You have a vivid imagination, Miss Stirling. But we can certainly look through all these boxes."

It was a boring process.

There were documents concerning land purchases and disposals, letters of contract, long details of marriage settlements and a host of other legal matters – but no paper with a description of how to find a hiding place.

Nothing that looked as though it could reveal the whereabouts of an unknown piece of treasure.

As Rupert began returning the documents to the last box, Celina was taking down several old books of estate records, only to be baffled as they seemed to be written in French.

Trying to put one back on its shelf, she misjudged the height and it fell from her grasp, splaying its pages over the stone floor.

She exclaimed, dismayed at having damaged such an ancient record.

"Not much harm done," Rupert calmed her, picking the book up and gathering up the pages before returning it to the shelf.

"But this seems to have come adrift."

Celina picked up a sheet of paper from the floor.

Rupert glanced at it, then opened the book again.

"This is written in a different hand. I don't think it belongs here," he muttered, showing her the creased pages.

"And, look, the paper is quite different, I think it must have been tucked into the book for some reason. Can you make out what it says?"

His closeness and the rapport that seemed to have developed between them while they were working together for a moment prevented Celina from looking properly at the sheet in front of her.

Then a sensation of betrayal towards the MacLeans rose inside her and she forced herself to try and interpret the difficult-to-read handwriting.

All the time she was conscious of Rupert leaning against the shelves and looking at her in a way that made her pulse race.

At last she raised her eyes from the document.

"It's all in French and beyond my command of the language. I think that it's been written a long time ago in medieval French and I don't recognise many of the words and phrases.

"But, look," she called out, suddenly excited, "here it talks of '*le trésor de la Croisade*'. '*Trésor*' is obviously 'treasure'. Do you think '*Croisade*' could be 'crusade'?"

"Not a word I came across in my French lessons, but it sounds likely. I haven't seen a dictionary here. Can you make out anything else?"

"No, but I do know who could. My Aunt Margaret. She has French ancestors and has always been interested in history. She has studied French archives and I am sure she could translate this for us."

He smiled at her.

"I like your use of the word '*us*'."

Celina blushed.

"We *are* working together over this business of the heirloom, is that not what you said?"

He nodded.

"Then let us take this piece of paper to Lady Bruce and ask if she will be so kind as to give us a translation. It is, after all, the first piece of evidence we have come across that this mythical heirloom might, after all, actually exist, even if no one knows where or what it is."

He left the room calling to Duncan for the trap to be harnessed.

"I hope you will not mind travelling this way," said Rupert, helping Celina into a small trap.

"It seems ridiculous for Duncan to have to drive us and Molly is tired after the trip to and from Drumlanrigg."

He stroked the neck of a sturdy brown horse.

"This is Jessie – she is younger and stronger."

"I am well used to travelling in this fashion," she replied, realising that she was pleased Duncan was not to drive them back to Drumlanrigg.

Rupert then climbed up beside her and set Jessie in motion.

"Tell me, my Lord, about life in America. From all I have heard it seems a very primitive place."

He gave an uninhibited laugh, then apologised.

"Please forgive me, but a comparison of New York bathrooms with those I have so far seen over here, which I must say are very few and far between, would reverse that judgement! But you are so right, once you start travelling West, life there can really be wild."

She settled back and listened with great interest to his tales of life in California and travelling around America helping his father build up his successful railway.

*

Dusk was falling as they reached Drumlanrigg.

"Now I very much hope you will stay here tonight, Lord Fitzalan," said Lady Bruce, welcoming them back. "You cannot find your way in the dark. Come in and tell me about what you have found – I can see that you are both excited about something."

Sitting in Lady Bruce's drawing room with a glass of whisky, Rupert recounted the results of their search.

"And we are hoping that you can help us," added Celina, bringing out the precious piece of paper.

She had carefully placed it between two sheets of card for the trip.

Lady Bruce studied the document.

"Yes, I don't see any trouble with this. It was most probably written in the sixteenth century."

She looked up at Celina.

"If I may abandon you, my guests, for a little, I will attempt a translation. Celina, my dear, you might want to change for dinner. Lord Fitzalan, since you have come all unprepared, you may be excused from changing, but I am sure you will want to refresh yourself after your exertions today. I will have you shown to your room."

He rose and gave his hostess a small bow.

"You are most kind, Lady Bruce. We left Castle Fitzalan in something of a hurry. I was anxious to reach here before the light gave out."

Lady Bruce smiled at him then grew serious.

"My dear Celina, I have to tell you that I have had a visit from Hamish this afternoon. Since you sent for your clothes and possessions, your presence in my household is known to the MacLeans. Normally I would have given you this news when we were alone, however I feel that, in the circumstances, Lord Fitzalan should hear what he had to say as well."

Celina felt herself grow pale.

"I am afraid that Hamish was quite intemperate and accused me of being a bad influence on you. He finished by saying that as you have now had long enough to recover from your hysteria – *his* word – you should return at once to Beaumarche. Oh, yes, and he left your engagement ring here for you."

Lady Bruce indicated where it sat on a side table in a silver dish.

Celina became angry.

How dare Hamish behave in such a manner?

How dare he suppose she would forget how he had behaved and meekly return to him?

"That ring can stay with him, Aunt Margaret. My engagement to Hamish MacLean is all over. What did you say to him?"

"That you were my guest for as long as you cared to stay and that you were presently out visiting, but would no doubt send word if you wished to see him."

"Oh, Aunt Margaret – that was perfect!"

"However, I do feel that young man may well take matters into his own hands – "

She looked at Celina and Rupert.

"I have asked my retainers to keep a watch for his presence on the estate, if he does appear, they are to inform him he should leave. Celina, I think you should not venture off Drumlanrigg for the time being and, you, Lord Fitzalan, will need to take extreme care when leaving us. We cannot be certain that Hamish MacLean does not receive word that you are visiting me."

Celina looked across at Rupert in alarm.

He gave her a reassuring smile.

"I am sure what Lady Bruce has said is for the best. I have taken the precaution of bringing my grandfather's shotgun with me. I shall not use it unless forced, but it may make young Hamish pause if he does try and accost me."

Celina gave out a small cry of distress and left the room.

She went to change with her emotions in turmoil.

How could she convince Hamish she would not in any circumstances renew her engagement to him?

And what would he do if he found out that she had spent the day in the company of Lord Fitzalan – and that he was to stay the night under the same roof as herself?

Would he believe that it was only to hunt down the wretched heirloom the MacLeans were claiming as theirs and that she hated and despised Lord Fitzalan?

Then she limply sat down on her bed.

No, she really had to admit to herself that today had taught her that Lord Fitzalan was certainly someone she could respect and even like.

When, however, had a Highland feud ever ended in anything but bloodshed?

*

After dinner, Lady Bruce produced her translation of the document Celina had discovered.

"It is the first page of a sixteenth century letter that was never sent, written by a Lady Fitzalan who, as was not uncommon was French, to her sister in Paris. It was at a time of much fighting between the Clans and her husband was embroiled in a bloody feud, though not, it seems with the MacLeans."

She smiled at Celina and Rupert.

"The letter writer was worried that Castle Fitzalan would fall in an attack that was imminent and they needed to hide the '*Crusade Treasure*'."

Celina gave a small cry of delight.

"Does she say what it was?"

"No, she just refers to it as the 'Crusade Treasure'. She goes on to write that it was to be hidden in an island tower in the loch below Castle Fitzalan."

Lady Bruce looked up from the document.

"I think I do know that loch on the Fitzalan estate. The island is quite small, but there *is* a tower on it."

"Does Lady Fitzalan describe exactly where it was to be hidden?" asked Rupert.

Lady Bruce shook her head.

"The letter breaks off. There is nothing to say if the attack actually took place or even if the 'Crusade Treasure' was indeed taken to the island."

"We know the Castle wasn't taken," mused Rupert, "but was the treasure hidden?"

"At least we can be certain that it exists," breathed Celina excitedly, then wished she had not spoken because Rupert added coldly,

"Are we to be sure? There is nothing to say it did not disappear after this letter was written – "

Celina felt a sense of depression come over her.

The rapport she had felt in the muniment room and on the ride back to Drumlanrigg seemed to have vanished.

Once again he was suspicious of her.

"However, this island and its tower must be closely searched. Lady Bruce, do you have a map of its location?"

A map was quickly found.

"It seems to be no further than a couple of hours' drive from here. I will go and explore it tomorrow."

"And *I* will come with you," stated Celina firmly.

"*No!*" replied Rupert even more firmly.

"Is that wise, Lord Fitzalan?" asked Lady Bruce.

"If you return and then declare the treasure was not there," Celina now turned towards Rupert, "Lord MacLean and Hamish will never believe you."

"You mean *you* will not believe me," he countered.

"Surely you don't mean that!" she cried, a wave of disappointment at his attitude flooding through her. "But you must see that a witness to whatever is or is not at that tower is essential."

Reluctantly Lady Bruce and Rupert finally agreed that she should accompany him.

*

Early the next morning, Celina dressed herself in warm clothes and before breakfast she packed a drawstring bag with everything she considered essential for the trip.

She had been surprised and shocked at how much she was disturbed by the realisation that Lord Fitzalan did not trust her.

She was determined somehow to prove that, while her deep loyalties might still belong to the MacLeans, she would not betray him.

When the trap was brought round, Rupert placed a shotgun within easy reach beneath a piece of tarpaulin,

They had left Drumlanrigg behind and were passing a wood when, suddenly, a group of riders emerged making eerie cries.

Celina could see with horror that the party was led by Lord MacLean.

He fired a shot that whistled past Rupert's head.

He whipped the horse into a faster pace and Celina seized the shotgun, brought it to her shoulder and pointed it at her uncle.

"Fall back," she cried.

He only laughed.

Her finger started to pull the trigger – but she found that she could not shoot at the man who had taken the place of her father over the last nine years.

In a moment the party had surrounded the trap.

Hamish leapt onto Rupert and Lord MacLean took the gun from Celina.

"Let him go, he is trying to find the heirloom," she howled, tears of frustration falling down her cheeks.

Several moments later Rupert was lying lifeless on the ground and Hamish had control of the reins.

"You are mine," he grated triumphantly to Celina as he brought the trap to a halt.

Lord MacLean swiftly dismounted and turned over Rupert's body.

"He's dead," he trumpeted. "He caught his head on one of those stones."

The world went dark and Celina knew no more.

CHAPTER FIVE

Pain shot viciously through Rupert's head.

At first he imagined that he had been attacked while walking home from his New York office.

Then realisation began to seep through.

He was not in New York, he had come to Scotland to take up his inheritance. But what was he doing lying on the ground, feeling as if his head had been battered in?

Memory gradually floated back.

He and Celina had been attacked on their way to try and locate this accursed heirloom that was causing all the trouble between him and the MacLeans.

She had taken up the shotgun and at first he thought she was going to shoot her uncle, but then she had lowered the gun. Hamish MacLean had jumped upon him and that was the last thing he remembered.

Managing to ignore the pain that seared through his head with the slightest movement, Rupert sat up.

Bright sun made his eyes ache, but it indicated that the trap stood nearby, the horse calmly cropping the grass.

For a moment he wondered why the MacLeans had gone, then realised that they must have left him for dead.

Celina Stirling must have gone with them.

Had she betrayed him?

Was her declaration last night that she no longer wished to be engaged to Hamish MacLean just a ruse?

Had she somehow managed to inform her relations where they were going?

He tried to dismiss this idea as nonsense, but found that it would not go away.

How long had he lain unconscious?

Looking at the sun, Rupert realised that it was at its height and several hours must have passed since the attack.

He staggered to his feet and managed to reach the trap. He held on to it for a while to allow his legs to regain some strength and then looked about him, searching for a stream he had noticed just before they were attacked – it was a little way off to his left.

Feeling stronger he went over and thrust his head into the cooling water. Blood still oozed from his wounds, but it did not seem all that serious.

He must be growing used to being assaulted!

On his way back from the stream, a flash of colour took him over to a gorse bush.

Tangled in it was a tartan scarf – it was Celina's and he carefully disentangled it to find that it was torn.

He felt both relief and anxiety.

Relief because surely the tear and the fact that the scarf had been abandoned suggested to him that she had been taken by force.

Anxiety that she, too, could have suffered injury.

Finding the scarf decided him.

He must rescue Celina from the MacLeans.

Jessie welcomed him with a friendly whinny and seemed not to have suffered in any way.

Rupert stood and stroked her neck while he tried to form a plan.

They had been attacked not far from Drumlanrigg,

so he was familiar with the lie of the land, particularly after studying Lady Bruce's map the previous evening.

He reckoned that he could find Beaumarche Castle without too much difficulty.

The shotgun had gone from the trap, but, thanks to Duncan, he was not exactly weaponless.

Jessie seemed quite happy to set out once again and trotted rapidly along. Finding the way, however, proved to be not as easy as Rupert had anticipated and he had to seek directions from a crofter before he eventually reached his destination.

Once at Beaumarche he had no difficulty in finding the place where Celina and he had emerged from the secret tunnel after she had rescued him.

As he tied Jessie to a convenient tree, he was more than ever certain that she must be in grave danger from the MacLeans.

Rupert felt a jolt of pain surge through him that had nothing to do with the blow he had suffered.

He could not bear to think of the beautiful girl who had released him from that dreadful dungeon when he was in the power of her vicious relatives.

A vision of her glorious red hair and the way her wide green eyes crinkled up when she smiled came to him.

He imagined her locked up in Beaumarche, perhaps even in the dungeon where he had been incarcerated.

He had to get to her as soon as possible.

He soon discovered the end of the tunnel behind the waterfall.

He opened the small iron grille and, with difficulty, entered the narrow passage, finally rising to his feet with relief as its height increased.

The pain in his head had now dulled into a nasty throbbing.

He reached the dungeon where he had been locked up. He forced himself to look inside and then realised with relief that it was empty.

Celina must be held elsewhere.

Moving as quietly as he could, Rupert climbed up the stone steps into the main part of the Castle and emerged behind the screen in the Great Hall.

The serving area that led to the kitchens was empty and Rupert stood still listening for any movement.

All seemed quiet.

In the dark distance he could hear the sounds of a drinking party. No doubt the MacLeans were celebrating a successful end to their expedition.

Well, soon Rupert would show them what crossing a Fitzalan could mean!

He peered through the carved screen into the Great Hall.

As he did so, a huge snore suddenly shook the air and he saw Lord MacLean and Hamish both slumped over the long refectory table.

Empty wine and whisky bottles were scatted around the two recumbent men and they had obviously celebrated the capture of Celina and his 'death' all too well!

He wondered where Celina might be held.

As he turned round and looked up a stone staircase that led into Beaumarche's tower, a servant came down the stairs, carrying linen over his arm.

He started back when he saw Rupert, but, before he could retreat, Rupert had one arm around the man's head, his hand stifling his cries.

With his other hand he held the knife Duncan had given him against the man's throat.

"Ye'll ken fine well yon *skean dhu* is such a trusty weapon," he had said, handing it over before Rupert set out to Drumlanrigg, "ye'll not ha' me with ye and I dinna trust those MacLeans. A gun is all very well, but a knife disn'a need reloading. Stick it in yer belt. If ye were wearing the kilt, it'd go into yer stocking, but a belt will be best for it."

"Take me to where Mistress Celina is being held," he hissed into the man's ear. "Or this will see your end."

The man dropped the linen he was holding and his eyes rolled frantically as he tried to nod.

Rupert transferred his grip from the man's mouth to his arm.

"One squeak out of you and you're a dead man," he growled.

The servant gulped and started up the stairs.

"My Lord, Miss Celina is not being held prisoner – she is free to come or go as she pleases."

Rupert saw this as a trick and kept hold of both the servant and his *skean dhu* as they climbed the stairs.

He opened a door – no key was necessary – forcing the servant into the room.

Celina was sitting in a wooden chair, gazing out of a window. No ropes bound her hands or arms, no shackles were on her feet and she was wearing the same clothes she had donned that morning.

"You have been quick, Thomas," she said without turning her head. "Put the clean linen on the bed and leave me."

The servant cleared his throat.

"Miss – " he stuttered, his voice a croak.

Celina turned and for a moment seemed transfixed.

"My – Lord?" she breathed as though he might be a phantom conjured up out of a Scottish mist.

Then she ran over to him.

"My Lord!" She held out both her hands to him. "I thought you were *dead*!"

She reached out as though to check his wound.

Rupert jerked his head back.

"As you can see, I am very much alive. I thought the MacLeans had kidnapped you and you were being held here against your will."

She gazed at him, looking bewildered.

"You mean – you came to rescue me?"

"He thought the Laird had locked you up, miss," gasped Thomas, trying to free himself from Rupert's grasp.

Rupert tightened his hold on the man's arm.

"I'll not have you raise the alarm," he said through gritted teeth.

He could not make sense of the situation.

If Celina was free, why was she here?

"Well, Mistress Stirling," he ground out. "What do you have to say for yourself? Did you come back here like a dog to its kennel?"

Her eyes blazed in sudden fury.

"How dare you question my presence here? Castle Beaumarche has been my home for more than ten years, where else should I go?"

"Why to Lady Bruce. You claimed that she was your refuge, that you could no longer bear to live with the MacLeans. Or was that all *a pretence*? A ruse to make me think I could trust you?"

Celina stared at him, her face white with shock.

"Once you knew where the treasure was hidden, did you alert the MacLeans and so lead me into an ambush this morning?"

"No!" she cried, her voice deep with anger. "If that had been the case, don't you think I would have taken them straight there, leaving you dead upon the moor?"

"If I was dead, you would not have to hurry to find that cursed heirloom."

The servant made another attempt to free himself and Rupert, angry with a sense of terrible disappointment, suddenly forced him to the ground, whipped the cover off the bed and bound it round him, making a helpless parcel of the man.

Then he gagged him with his own handkerchief and flung him onto the bed.

"There, that will keep you from raising any alarm. Do I need to do the same to *you*?" he snarled at Celina.

Every line in her body spoke of frustrated fury.

"I could almost wish you had been killed and were lying dead by that road. Cannot you understand that I want nothing more than to bring this stupid feud to an end?"

Suddenly a thought seemed to strike her.

"What have you done with my uncle and Hamish?"

"Nothing."

"They would not have allowed you to walk up here without a fight. I cannot imagine how you beat them off. Did you take them by surprise? Have you killed them?"

She sounded distraught.

He smiled grimly.

"There was no fight, Celina. You say you want to end this feud by finding the heirloom. Will you then prove it by coming with me now?"

She gulped hard and looked steadily at him.

"If you can prove to me that you have not harmed my uncle and cousin – yes, I will."

"Then follow me."

Rupert started down the stone staircase and then he realised that Celina was not behind him, and turned back to find she was picking up the drawstring bag she had taken with her when they set out from Drumlanrigg.

"Go before me," ordered Rupert.

Much as he wanted to, he did not feel he could trust Celina Stirling.

"What about Thomas? We can't leave him bound up like that."

"He will soon be able to free himself, as I did no more than wrap him up. Now – move on."

He spoke to her more harshly than he had intended and heard her take a quick inward breath.

He followed her down the stone staircase.

At the bottom he whispered,

"If you look through the screen, you will see your uncle and cousin both sprawled across the table, happily inebriated!"

She walked up to the screen.

"They look dead!" she murmured, alarmed.

Then she recoiled as two deafening snores assured her they were indeed very much alive.

With a sound of disgust she exclaimed,

"No need for you to defend yourself against them for the moment! They will not stir for several hours."

"It is not the first time you have seen them in this state, then?"

"It is really their idea of how to celebrate. I – " she hesitated for a few seconds, "I have always found it such a repellent habit. They see it as behaving like brave Scots Highlanders."

"The sounds from the kitchen suggest the servants are downing alcohol with equal delight, perhaps if we walk out of the main door, no one will stop us."

She looked curiously at him.

"Did you not enter that way?"

"Indeed not. I expected to find the place armed and ready to withstand an invading force. I came by the tunnel route. Jessie and the trap are where you left Prince."

"Ah, of course! I think, however, we don't need to use it now. We will leave via the garden."

She walked past the two drunken men splayed over the table and Rupert followed her into another part of the house that must have been built later and had more charm than the Great Hall.

Celina opened a side door onto a pretty garden and they struck out across a lawn and through a yew hedge.

It did not take them very long to come to where the horse and trap had been left.

As they reached it, Rupert placed his right hand on her shoulder.

"Mistress Stirling, are you certain that you wish to accompany me to the island?"

She looked back towards him, her eyes filled with an unidentifiable emotion.

"I wish you could believe you can trust me."

He returned her gaze for a long moment, feeling he was almost drowning in those lovely eyes and wishing the moment could go on for ever.

Slowly he nodded.

"I do want to trust you, Celina."

She closed her eyes and gave a deep sigh.

"I am glad," she responded simply.

He looked up at the sun, now low in the sky.

"I think that we should better leave the island until tomorrow. We will return now to Drumlanrigg."

Nothing else was said as they drove to Lady Bruce.

"My dears," she greeted them. "How glad I am to see you back. Have you found it?"

"I regret, Aunt Margaret, that again my wretched and perverse uncle and cousin decided to mount an attack. Lord Fitzalan sustained a nasty injury and I think it should receive some medical attention."

Immediately Lady Bruce was all concern and called for warm water, clean towels and salve.

But when they arrived, it was Celina who insisted on attending to his wound.

"Nasty, but I think it will soon mend," she said as she bathed it.

He flinched as, despite the gentleness of her touch, pain seared through his head.

After cleaning the injury, she applied a salve.

"No need for any bandage. It has stopped bleeding and air will assist the healing process."

"Now," suggested Lady Bruce with great authority, "you must tell me exactly what has happened."

Rupert allowed Celina to tell the story.

He leaned back in his chair and watched her face as she gave brief details.

Could he really trust her?

She had come with him willingly enough, but would she turn on him once they found the heirloom?

If indeed they did find it?

"Well, now, that's quite a tale," their hostess added once it was finished. "What a very stupid man your Uncle Robert is, Celina. I hope you told him just how stupid?"

Celina nodded, a flush rising to her cheeks.

"Lord Fitzalan looked as though – he was dead and Uncle Robert told me that he was. I – well – it was such a shock! It all happened so quickly. One moment we were trotting happily along and the next we were surrounded by MacLeans. I hit Uncle Robert with my fists and called him some dreadful names."

"I should think you did and in what state is he now? Did he try to stop you leaving this second time?"

Celina shook her head.

"When we returned to Beaumarche, he said that I must now know where the heirloom was hidden and should take them to it. I refused."

"You did not deny you knew its location?" Rupert quizzed her, again feeling that his trust in her was slipping away.

Celina shrugged.

"I preferred to tell him that I would not help in any way."

"But if you thought Lord Fitzalan was dead," asked Lady Bruce, "what harm could there be in telling them?"

A red flush appeared on Celina's cheeks.

"And let the MacLeans benefit so fully from their treacherous behaviour? I could not allow that and I am surprised, Aunt Margaret, that you think I might have."

Lady Bruce then inclined her head in apology and Rupert admired Celina's spirit.

If she spoke the truth, she was a remarkable girl. If only he could trust her!

He realised he wanted to do so above all else.

"So when we reached Beaumarche and they called for alcohol, I took myself to my room. By the time Lord Fitzalan regained consciousness and had made his way to Beaumarche, Uncle Robert and Hamish had drunk so much they were out cold and he had no need to defend himself – thank Heavens."

"I am not one to countenance heavy drinking, but in this instance, it has undoubtedly saved further bloodshed!"

Lady Bruce now looked at both of them.

"What will you do tomorrow?"

"Take another road to that loch," answered Rupert promptly. "Can you find us a different way, Lady Bruce?"

The map was once again produced and his hostess showed him how he could take a more circuitous route – it would take somewhat longer, but it was one no one would suspect him of taking.

"We should start even earlier tomorrow morning," suggested Celina.

Rupert looked up from the map warily.

"You still intend coming with me?"

"Of course. I mean to see an end to this feud."

He looked at her beautiful and determined face and knew he longed to be able to see her without this wretched question of trust hanging over them.

He hoped fervently that the next day would see the end of their search.

CHAPTER SIX

Celina looked at Rupert and realised that, despite what he had said beside the trap that afternoon, he still did not altogether trust her.

But in turn could she trust him?

Had he really believed she was being held captive by her uncle and Hamish?

Had he come to Beaumarche because he felt that he owed it to her for rescuing him from that dungeon?

If he had wanted to kill her uncle and cousin he had ample opportunity with both of them in a drunken stupor, but she did not really think he was capable of such an act.

She went upstairs to change her gown.

It was a relief to escape Rupert's scrutiny.

He had such a strong face and such magnetic eyes.

Celina knew she wanted to trust him and the steady gaze of those eyes.

If only he trusted *her*!

But how could he when her relations behaved so disgracefully?

For so many years Celina had accepted her Uncle Robert and Cousin Hamish as roistering men who were full of life and excitement.

They had helped her accept the tragic death of her parents and to build another life for herself. Believing that she was in love with Hamish as they grew up could be seen as a normal development from all the fun and affection that they had shared together over so many years.

Celina changed into an evening gown of bronze silk and tried to sort out her tangled emotions.

Initially she had hated Rupert not because she had been told to, but because of the revelation he had brought when her eyes had been opened so brutally as to the true nature of her uncle and cousin.

Horror had filled her when she saw the way they had treated their prisoner.

Her own sense of honour had meant she had to help him escape, even though she believed she still hated him.

Since he had arrived at her Godmother's, she had gradually been forced to change her opinion.

The attack on the trap and the shock of hearing her uncle declare that Lord Fitzalan was dead after Hamish had thrown him to the ground had been devastating.

No wonder she had lost consciousness.

It had only been for a few moments and when she had come to, the MacLeans had tried to get her to disclose where she and Lord Fitzalan had been going.

The more she had refused, the more determined her Uncle Robert had become. Finally he struck her across the face and ordered Hamish to take her up on his horse. They were all to return to Beaumarche.

"But what about *him*?" Celina had cried, pointing at the lifeless figure on the ground.

Lord MacLean scrutinised her closely.

"Why on earth should you care what happens to a dead man?" he grated. "The carrion crows will deal with his body!"

His callousness made Celina speechless.

She resisted Hamish's attempt to pull her onto his horse and ran for the trap.

"I will take his body back to Castle Fitzalan, then," she shouted.

Hamish caught her and cuffed her around the head.

"Try that again and I will tie you up and sling you over the back of my horse," he snarled with a laugh.

Bruised and faint and her head swimming with the force of his blow, Celina could see no alternative to going to Beaumarche.

On arrival she went straight to her room, followed by the voice of Hamish saying to his father in a cruel voice,

"I'll *drag* the information out of her!"

He forced his way into her room and threatened her with the same treatment they had given Lord Fitzalan if she didn't tell them where they had been going.

Celina had stubbornly refused.

Although she noticed his hands itched to strike her, it seemed he could understand that a beating was not going to help his cause.

Finally he told her that she had until that evening to change her mind.

After Hamish had left her, Celina tried to reconcile the cruel behaviour of the MacLeans with her memories of life with them since the death of her parents.

Was it their current money worries that had brought these violent urges to the surface or had the terrible rages and cruelty always been present?

Comments heard from some of the retainers on odd incidents that she had ignored before came back to her now and she decided the MacLeans had taken care to shield her from this odious side of their characters.

She tried to forget the picture of Rupert's body, that vibrant figure drained of his life and slaughtered by her relations.

It was then she realised how much she had enjoyed the time spent in his company.

She thought how wonderful it would have been if together they had found the heirloom and managed to solve its ownership and so bring this horrible feud to an end.

A vital force had disappeared from her life and she realised for the first time how much she had been attracted to this Scot who spoke with a slight American accent.

She wondered if she would have mourned as much if it had been Hamish who had died.

When Rupert had appeared in her room, at first she thought he must be a ghost.

When she realised that he was really alive, Celina had felt an overwhelming delight flood through her veins as she fully recognised how much poorer her life would be without him.

Almost immediately, however, he had accused her of betraying him to the MacLeans.

Much of her joy had then drained away and a deep bitterness took its place.

Even as she swore that he was wrong, Celina once again almost hated him for making her understand the true nature of the MacLeans.

When she saw the two men spread-eagled over the table, their drunken state disgusted her.

She fastened a topaz necklace around her neck and checked her appearance.

Her hated freckles were particularly prominent that evening and her hair was a storm of electricity around her face. She ran her fingers through it in frustration.

She wanted to look her most attractive this evening.

But why, when Lord Fitzalan did not trust her?

She went downstairs in a dangerous mood.

Almost immediately, however, Rupert disarmed her by rising to his feet as she entered the room.

"Allow me to say how beautiful you look tonight, Mistress Stirling!"

The slight American accent that seemed to slow his words gave them additional force.

"Aye, she's a bonnie lass," agreed Lady Bruce,

At dinner Lady Bruce coaxed him into telling them about New York, and Celina found herself fascinated by his account of a bustling, rapidly-growing City.

Then he paused and looked at Celina,

"You must think it all sounds really rather vulgar compared with all the serenity and beauty of the Scottish countryside!"

Celina laughed, her mood now in tune with his.

"Serenity! How can you, my Lord, talk about peace and harmony in such a place where you have twice been attacked by feuding natives!"

"Ah, but as well I have been rescued by a beautiful young lady and then introduced to a most gracious Scottish aristocrat," he added at once, giving Lady Bruce a bow.

Lady Bruce smiled.

"Not all our ancient families are as contentious and pig-headed – I hope, Celina my dear, you will not mind my referring to your MacLean Clan as pig-headed. Though I have to admit that they are not the only ones. The history of the Highlands is littered with feuds between Clans, but we must not spoil our pleasant evening by going into such matters. Lord Fitzalan, do tell us more about America."

By the time they retired for the night, Celina found herself longing to visit a country so huge that she could not take in the time it took to travel from one side to the other.

She wanted to see the vast variety of scenery. She went to sleep trying to imagine what the Rocky Mountains and the Grand Canyon actually looked like and how it felt to see giant redwood trees and the Pacific Ocean.

Would she ever, she found herself wondering, have the opportunity to travel to the USA?

*

Very early the following morning, they set out on their second attempt to visit the island in the loch.

Celina had once again put on a plain kersey dress with a warm scarf around her shoulders with stout shoes on her feet.

A visit to Lady Bruce's housekeeper had provided her with a bag full of food. Also in there was the revolver she had brought with her when she had first sought refuge with Lady Bruce.

Lord MacLean and Hamish might yet have cause to regret they had taught her excellent marksmanship!

It was a lovely day, fresh with bright sun promising later warmth.

As Rupert drove the horse and trap, Celina enjoyed asking him more about his life in America. Gradually she learnt how the American Railroad Company that he and his father had built had made them wealthy.

Maybe he had no need of the heirloom for funds to restore Castle Fitzalan.

"How can you spend time in Scotland?" she asked. "Aren't you afraid that the Company is falling apart back in America?"

He glanced round at her, a smile lighting his eyes in a way that made her heart jump in an oddly crazy way, a way she not experienced even when Hamish had asked her to marry him.

"I have every confidence in an excellent deputy and a great team. And cablegrams can keep me in touch with what is going on."

Celina looked around them at the bare moors they were travelling over.

"Cablegrams?"

He laughed.

"I have to admit I did not realise quite how far from any town Castle Fitzalan is. I may have to install my own cable line."

For a moment she thought he was joking.

When she appreciated that he was not, she realised just how rich he must be, and that it was ridiculous of Lord MacLean to think that this Fitzalan could be interested in depriving him of an heirloom, no matter how valuable.

Then his mouth tightened.

"Your Uncle Robert has no idea what he has taken on with this feud. I owe it to my grandfather not to let this treasure, whatever it is, out of my hands without *absolute* proof that it does not belong to the Fitzalans."

Celina felt a shiver down her spine.

Suddenly Rupert brought the trap to a halt.

"There," he cried. "Surely that is the loch?"

In the distance water gleamed in the sunlight.

It was not too long before they reached the loch. A rough road ran beside the water and in the distance was an island.

As they drew closer Celina could make out a tower.

"It must be the tower mentioned in the letter," she blurted out excitedly, "but it seems almost a ruin."

Rupert nodded his head.

"Not in good shape, I would admit. It's very hard to imagine anything of value being hidden there."

"But perhaps the tower was fine when it was – "

He gave Celina a grin.

"I like a girl with imagination."

He looked at the island again.

"We shall need a boat to reach the island."

A little further down the road there was a cottage.

Outside it, Rupert gave the reins to Celina, jumped down and was soon speaking to a wizened crofter.

"Ye can hire me boat," he said, coming to the trap. "But I'll not take ye meself. That there tower is haunted."

He looked at Celina with rheumy old eyes.

"*Haunted*?"

"Aye, lassie. Many, many years ago, long afore I were born, that tower were in fine shape and an old crazed man lived there."

Celina looked across at Rupert and knew that, like her, he was thinking that this crofter looked old and crazed himself!

"His daughter would daily row o'er with food and drink. One evening when she was settin' off back, others came. Words were exchanged and then blows. Both killed they were, the old man and his daughter. Ever since then the tower has stood empty."

"Who does it belong to?" asked Rupert.

"Why, to the Fitzalans. Them who lives yonder."

The old crofter waved a hand over to the other side of the loch.

"Big castle they has. But the old Laird's not been here this many a year."

"And who is supposed to have killed the old man and his daughter?" asked Celina with a sinking feeling that she already knew the answer.

The crofter shook his head slowly.

"They don't say, but some would swear it were the MacLeans. At any rate since that time, the place has been cursed. There are those who've seen lights flickerin' in the tower and who swear," he lowered his voice dramatically, "they've seen the ghosts of the slaughtered walking on the island. Ye'll not get me out there, lassie!"

He shuddered, seemingly genuinely afraid.

Celina felt an irrational dread run down her spine.

"If you'll be so good as to show us where you keep your boat, we'll row ourselves across," suggested Rupert, producing enough coins to make the crofter's eyes gleam with delight.

They were led down to the water's edge and shown where a small rowing boat was hitched to a tree stump.

"We should not be too long. Will you unharness my horse and let it graze while we are on the island?"

The old crofter nodded.

Rupert looked at Celina.

"Are you game for a row, Miss Stirling? Or would you prefer to remain here and wait for me to confirm there is nothing hidden in the tower?"

Another shudder ran down Celina's spine.

Could she trust him? She knew he did not trust her, no matter how friendly he seemed.

Haunted island or no, she must go with him.

Soon they were in the boat and pulling at their oars with a matching rhythm, Rupert looking over his shoulder from time to time to ensure they were heading in the right direction.

"You have done this before," Celina quizzed him.

"Of course. We have rivers and lakes in America, you know."

He sounded hurt, but she smiled,

"You have told me such a lot about your Railway Company I can only associate you with trains!"

Several minutes later the bow of the boat bumped into the island. Rupert leapt out and held the boat steady for Celina to step out.

At close quarters the condition of the tower seemed even more ramshackle than it had from the mainland.

Stones were missing, the top looked as frayed as an old blanket and shuttered windows empty of glass looked blindly over the loch.

"I wonder what this tower was for," mused Rupert. "It hardly seems large enough for a permanent habitation, nor secure enough for defence."

"Perhaps it was an outpost," suggested Celina, "for guards to watch for the approach of an enemy."

She looked up at the stressed grey stone and felt an atmosphere of chilling doom about the place.

"An outpost – I like the sound of that."

Rupert went up to the sturdy wood door and turned the ring that did service for a handle.

"It's locked!" he exclaimed in surprise.

"The door looks strong," Celina said doubtfully as he tried to force an entrance. "Perhaps there is a key – "

He gave a shout of laughter.

"A key? My dear girl, do you really expect to find it hanging here on the wall, ready for anyone to make their entrance?"

He sounded so good-humoured that she could not take offence, so she riposted,

"Many people hide one beneath a stone!"

For a moment she thought that he would class that as ridiculous too. Instead he began to search beneath some of the largish stones that stood around the tower.

They looked as if they could well have fallen from the top and she could not imagine they would provide any sort of secure hiding place.

She walked round the tower.

On its other side there was a stone bench that faced South. She sat on it and held her face up to the sun, feeling its warmth dismiss some of the doom-laden atmosphere.

A little family of ducks sailed out from the edge of the island.

Celina rose and went to investigate.

A small inlet had been lined with building stones and there they had made a nest.

After smiling at the sight of the ducks, she looked at the stones more closely.

Then she grasped the top of one of them, gave it a strong jerk and found herself holding on to what could only be described as a lid.

Someone in the past had hollowed out a stone and found or fashioned a flat one to sit securely on its top.

And there inside was a large and ancient iron key!

She grabbed it and ran back to the other side of the tower. Rupert was still picking up stones and hurling them down again in mounting frustration.

"I've found it!"

"Good Heavens. What a wonderful girl you are."

He regarded her with a beaming smile and all over again she felt her heart give an extraordinary lurch.

"Now let's see if we can persuade that old lock to turn."

It took a little time, but he patiently worked the key and finally gave a grunt of triumph.

"It's giving!"

A moment later he put his shoulder to the door and gave it a steady push.

With a resounding creak, it ground open.

They could now enter!

CHAPTER SEVEN

Rupert led the way in.

The interior of the tower was as tumbledown as the exterior. In the curious way of some ancient buildings, it seemed larger on the inside than the outside.

It certainly appeared roomy enough to be used as a home, although Rupert reckoned every gust of wind and drop of rain would penetrate to the interior and make living there miserable.

"How dark it is," commented Celina.

She went over to one of the windows and struggled to open one of the shutters. Finally it creaked free of years of clinging dirt and immediately rays of sunshine showed up the crumbling walls and layers of dust on the floor, as a rickety table and two broken chairs were the only furniture.

On the far wall was an open fireplace, a large bread oven to its left side. A dangerously unstable stone staircase led up to the next floor, which must offer a single room the same size as this one.

Recalling the many windows on the outside, Rupert thought there was probably yet another floor.

"Could the stone oven offer a hiding place?" asked Celina doubtfully. "But if this tower was searched when the old man and his daughter were killed, surely that's the first place they would look. Maybe, however, that attack was not anything to do with the hidden heirloom."

Rupert found himself watching her nimble grace as she walked over and pulled open the oven's door.

So would angels walk on clouds! He gave himself a mental shake and dismissed such thoughts.

Celina gave a sigh of disappointment.

"There's only twigs and more dust."

Then she stuck her head inside for a closer look.

"Do you think there could be a secret place at the back of it, my Lord?"

Rupert took a cursory look.

"We need some light. Why didn't I think of it?" he added, cross with himself that he had not brought candles.

"I may be able to help."

Celina went to collect the bag she had brought with her, undid the tie top and rummaged around inside.

"Here we are."

She took out several candles and a box of matches.

"All provided by Aunt Margaret's housekeeper and she has also produced some food."

She lit a candle and, holding it, once again inserted her head in the oven for a closer look.

Rupert was horrified.

"It's not safe," he called urgently, pulling her back, terrified her wonderful red hair would catch fire.

Feeling her slim waist beneath his hands sent such an unexpected jolt of electricity through him that Rupert released her as though she was already on fire.

"You are welcome to check yourself, but there does not seem to be any hidden cupboard," said Celina, her face flushed.

"Please, Celina, forgive me – for removing you so unceremoniously, but you put yourself in such danger," he stammered awkwardly.

She gave a gurgle of laughter, her eyes lively and sparkling.

"You are too much the gentleman, and I give you full permission to rescue me from any perilous situation!"

Rupert swept her a low bow, his heart lifting at her teasing.

"Thank you indeed, Mistress Stirling, I hereby now appoint myself your bodyguard!"

He took the candle from her and stuck his own head in the oven, sweeping the flame carefully around the worn bricks. There was no sign of any secret hiding place.

He emerged and blew out the candle.

He was about to admit that Celina had been right when he saw that she was mounting the stairs.

"No!" he cried.

The steps were in such a ruinous condition that one could collapse under even her slight weight and there was no rail to prevent her falling back onto the stone floor.

Celina laughed and continued her way up.

Rupert did not dare to follow her, realising that his greater weight could trigger exactly the sort of catastrophe he feared.

With his heart in his mouth he watched her climb.

She was nearly at the top when a step gave way.

Her hands reached for a support that would prevent her falling ten or more feet onto the unforgiving flagstones.

There was nothing.

Rupert had been prepared and managed to catch her, but not before she had caught her head on the sharp edge of one of the steps.

Celina's body felt as light as a bird, but in a heart-stopping moment he realised she had been knocked out.

The table looked too rickety to bear even her slim body so he placed gently her onto the lowest step, stripped off his jacket, folded it and laid it beneath her head.

He smoothed back the hair from her forehead and tried to see where she was wounded. There did not seem to be any blood but he could feel a swelling.

For one terrible moment he wondered whether she had suffered damage to her brain.

The thought that this girl, who seemed more alive than any he had ever met, might never again give him her most sparkling smile, never again walk with her light steps, never again look so sweetly serious as she worried about the feud her uncle and cousin were carrying on with him, was so devastating he almost groaned out loud.

He went and soaked his handkerchief in the loch, then carefully spread it over her forehead.

After a moment she gave a moan and stirred a little.

Full of hope Rupert willed her to open her eyes.

He did not know what had happened to him, but he was certain he had never cared so much about a girl before.

How could Celina Stirling have inveigled her way into his heart when he suspected she was deceiving him?

When it seemed more than possible she intended to use him to locate the heirloom for her MacLean relations, how could he find himself so attracted to her?

Her eyelids fluttered lightly, she lifted a hand to her forehead and moaned again and then opened her eyes and looked straight into his.

"What – happened?" she mumbled.

Rupert forgot all his doubts as his heart overflowed with relief.

"You were nearly at the top of the steps when one gave way and you fell."

There was a little smile as she whispered,

"You did warn me – not to climb up them – didn't you?"

He nodded in agreement.

She said nothing more for a moment and he waited, wondering if it was still too soon to rejoice that she did not seem to have suffered any serious damage.

"My head hurts," she moaned.

"You caught it on a sharp edge as you fell. Shall I rinse the handkerchief in fresh water for you?"

She gave a slight nod and he dashed outside again, glad that he had a clean handkerchief with him.

By the time he returned, Celina had managed to sit herself upright.

"You should stay lying down," he advised gently.

She gave him a faint smile.

"I like being up and about – "

Her voice seemed stronger now and he arranged the wet linen on her forehead and held her wrist to feel her pulse. Perhaps it was a little faster than it should have been but only a little.

Rupert finally allowed himself to hope that she was going to be all right.

He rearranged his jacket on the step behind her so it provided a comfortable support.

Then he went and leant against the window, hands in his pockets studying her and alert for any change in her condition.

"You caught me when I fell?" Celina enquired, her voice a little stronger now.

He nodded his head.

She put a hand to her forehead as he removed the damp handkerchief.

"You have saved my life," she sighed wonderingly. "If you hadn't caught me – I would probably have broken my neck."

She looked up to the top of the steps and then at the flagstones and shuddered.

"You could have left me lying, dead or dying, while you looked for the heirloom. Then, if you'd found it, you could have hidden it somewhere else and gone for help too late to save me and told everyone we could not find it."

Rupert straightened up, horrified at what she was saying.

"How could you even think that!" Rupert sounded appalled. "No one would do such a dastardly thing."

"No?" She gave him a curious look. "I could name you some who would!"

He knew she was referring to the MacLeans.

Then he remembered his suspicions about her.

"I am ashamed to say," she went on in a low voice, "that I have wondered whether I could trust you fully."

She lifted her head and her gaze met his.

"Now I know that you are honourable and that you will not try to deceive me."

Her frankness was so attractive, he wanted to rush over and draw her into his arms.

Instead he now felt that he should, in return for her confession, admit to his own doubts about her.

He squared his shoulders and took a deep breath.

But before he could speak, his eye was caught by the displaced stone Celina had fallen from.

"Good Heavens," he cried and leaped athletically onto the stairs two steps above where she was sitting.

"Please, do be careful," Celina implored him. "You have seen how dangerous these stairs are."

He then stopped short of the point where Celina had fallen.

From below he had seen that, when it slipped, the stone that had caused Celina's fall had revealed a gap.

Through it he could see some sort of metal lever.

Testing his weight on the step to ensure it was firm enough, Rupert tried to grasp the lever.

Too much mortar was in the way.

He then drew Duncan's *skean dhu* from his belt and started to scrape the mortar away.

He was conscious of Celina leaning against the wall at the foot of the stairs watching him, one hand held up to her mouth as though she feared for his safety.

At first gradually and then more quickly, the mortar fell away.

At last Rupert could put his hand around the lever and pull it towards him.

There was a gasp from Celina as, with a rumble, the step above swung outwards, forcing Rupert down a step to avoid being thrown off the stairs.

"What has happened?"

"Keep back," urged Rupert as she started to climb up. "I don't want you falling again."

The movement of the stone had uncovered a large and dark hole. Such a sophisticated device could only have been installed to provide a place where something of great value would be concealed.

Rupert felt carefully inside.

Almost immediately he gave a grunt of satisfaction.

"What have you found?" asked Celina urgently.

He gently lifted out an ancient leather satchel and cradling it in his arms, he came back down the stairs.

Celina was watching him, holding out her arms as though to catch him if he should stumble.

"Do you think this could possibly hold the treasure that has caused so much trouble?" he mused as he reached the ground.

She gave him a warm smile.

"There is only one way to find out."

He grinned back and put the satchel on the table.

The leather straps were so old it proved impossible to release them through their rusted clasps.

Rupert brought out the *skean dhu* again and sawed through each strap. It took a heartbreakingly long time.

Inside was an object wrapped in woollen plaid.

Rupert looked at Celina.

"Would you like to undertake the honours, Mistress Stirling?"

She was startled.

"Do you not want to reveal it yourself?"

"You were honest enough, Celina, to tell me that before your fall you had not been able to trust me. I now have to admit that, despite all you did to free me from the threats of your relatives, I did not feel able to trust *you*."

Celina looked as shocked as he had felt when she made her confession.

"I do, however, trust you completely now and as a token of that trust, I want it to be you to reveal whatever is inside that fabric."

She looked at him for a long moment.

As the silence lengthened, Rupert was feeling more and more nervous.

Then Celina gave him a warm smile.

"We have both been fools. Shall we agree that all suspicion is now in the past?"

Rupert thrust out his hand.

"Let us shake on it."

Celina's eyes twinkled.

"Shall we use your knife to mingle our blood and so seal the pact?"

For a moment Rupert felt a jolt of passion.

Then she laughed.

"We are not children. Our words do not need blood to be sincere and binding."

She took his hand and gravely shook it.

"Trust and honesty between us, *yes*?"

He nodded, his gaze fixed on hers.

A slight flush came to her cheeks.

Then reverently Celina lifted up the bundle, placed it on the table and began to unwrap the contents.

As the last of the fabric fell away, both Rupert and Celina gasped.

Standing on the table before them was a *gold cup*.

It had a shallow bowl with two handles. Its short stem was broken by a round knob and was set onto a broad base.

The cup was not very large and its only decoration was an incised pattern around the rim, but the proportions and the skill with which it had been made were such that it was one of the most beautiful objects Rupert had ever seen.

Celina sighed as she looked at it.

"It's lovely," she breathed. "Surely it's a *chalice*?"

Rupert nodded.

"My father collected several from various ages. He said that he liked to think of priests taking communion and handling these precious vessels so many centuries ago. He felt they were a living link with a sacred past."

Celina put out a hand.

"May I touch it?" she asked in an awed voice.

Rupert picked up the chalice and gave it to her.

"There – now we have both touched it."

He watched her turn it in her hand so that she could admire the interlaced patterns running around the rim.

It was about seven inches in height and some nine inches in diameter.

"It looks as though it could hold a lot of wine," she reflected after a moment.

Rupert sighed and then began to speculate,

"So maybe it originally belonged to a large Church or even a Cathedral. It is like one in my father's collection that he claimed was from the twelfth or thirteenth century, possibly from Constantinople or Jerusalem. I just wonder how it came to belong to a Scottish family?"

As he spoke, Rupert looked inside the satchel.

"Hello, there's something else in here."

He extracted a piece of crumpled paper.

"Maybe this will tell us something."

After scrutinising it for a few moments, he handed the paper to Celina.

"I think it is written in Gaelic. I seem to recognise one or two words, but I don't know enough of the language to be able to understand what it says."

She put down the cup and took the piece of paper.

"It's a little difficult to read, but I think I can make out the gist."

Celina sat down on one of the chairs, frowning over the paper.

"How is your head?" Rupert asked her.

She smiled absently.

"Getting better by the minute!"

Rupert sat nervously on the other chair, afraid his weight might prove too much for its rickety condition, but it seemed to hold up and he enjoyed gazing at Celina as she sat there studying the document.

She was somewhat pale but otherwise seemed to be recovering well.

The fact that each of them had admitted to a lack of trust in the other seemed to have cleared the air.

He felt totally at ease with her and hoped fervently that it was now the same for her.

At last she looked up from the paper.

"The chalice was brought back from the Holy Land by a Scottish Crusader. It was apparently sold to him for funds to feed the starving poor."

"It must have been something like that. I am sure that no Christian would have stolen it," commented Rupert, staring at the lovely treasure.

"By tradition it has to be handed down from eldest son to eldest son – "

"So it *is* an heirloom."

"Indeed, and this paper goes on to state that if there is no male heir of the Beaumarche line – "

Celina stopped and looked at Rupert.

He knew what she was thinking – that the heirloom must belong to the MacLeans.

"If there is no male Beaumarche heir," she went on, "then it has to go to the Crown of Scotland. I'm so sorry, my Lord, as Beaumarche is the MacLean ancestral home, it would seem that this heirloom belongs to them."

Rupert thought for a moment.

"I don't think we can take that for granted," he said eventually.

Celina's expression then darkened and he wondered if the trust between them was already beginning to fracture.

"Let me think," Rupert began again. "It may well be, however, that Lord MacLean is the rightful heir to the Beaumarche line, but just because his family has passed down a property of that name, does not automatically mean that he, too, is a Beaumarche.

"If so then why is he not called Beaumarche? My grandfather must have had some grounds for believing that the heirloom belonged to him, even though his name was not Beaumarche either. After all, the document we found that sent us to this place was in a *Fitzalan* record book."

He paused, thinking hard.

"I remember seeing a book in the muniments room with a family tree. It didn't seem relevant at the time, but now it could well solve the mystery of why neither of our families is called Beaumarche."

"Then we should both go back to Castle Fitzalan at once," Celina suggested decisively.

She put the paper on the table beside the chalice.

"How wonderful it is we have found the heirloom and are so near to discovering the rightful owner.

"I do hope," she added impulsively, "that it turns out to be *you*."

"My only hope is that the truth will end this stupid feud for ever," asserted Rupert soberly.

"And mine too," agreed Celina fervently.

Quietly they then wrapped up the chalice again and placed it back in the satchel.

As Rupert added the piece of paper, Celina asked,

"I just wonder why the document we found at your Castle was written in French and this one was in Gaelic."

"Are they both in the same hand?"

Celina took out the paper and looked at it again.

"I don't think so."

"Then each writer probably used the language they were most familiar with. We know the other document was written by a French woman. Probably this was written by another member of the family – maybe one who was more comfortable using Gaelic.

"If they were afraid that the Castle might fall to an enemy, they must have been under great pressure. It would make sense to cut down the amount of time it would take to prepare both documents."

"Oh, yes!" she cried, "I can see how it must have been. The courtyard filled with people rushing to and fro trying to prepare a few necessities to take with them if they had to flee and secreting precious items away."

There was a far away look in her eyes as though she had been transported back in time.

"And no doubt some trusted servant was given the satchel and told to go and hide it here in the tower."

"The hiding place must have been prepared some time before. In those far-off times I would suppose many people would have devised some safe and secret place to protect the most precious of their possessions."

The document went back into the satchel with the chalice.

"Are you sure you are able to come with me to the Castle?" Rupert asked Celina. "Would it not be better for me to take you back to Drumlanrigg? You cannot quite have recovered from that blow to your head."

She put up a hand and felt the bump under her hair.

"It is still sore, but I am not suffering in any other way, I assure you, my Lord. Come let's now row back and return the boat to its owner. Something is telling me that we should reach Castle Fitzalan as soon as possible."

CHAPTER EIGHT

The blow to Celina's head ached more than she was prepared to admit to Rupert, but she managed to row in a matching rhythm with him as they crossed the loch.

She looked back at the tower receding gradually as they slid across the dark water.

The sun had gone and clouds were massing. They would be lucky to reach Castle Fitzalan before rain fell.

The satchel lay in the bottom of the boat between their feet.

Despite her pain, she found herself visualising the lovely golden cup they had found.

It really was a treasure.

How much would the MacLeans desire the chalice once they knew exactly what it was and what it could be worth?

Celina knew that Rupert himself did not care what the chalice was worth as it was its sheer beauty and what it represented that appealed to him.

The MacLeans would never appreciate its beauty – only what it could be sold for.

She glanced at Rupert sitting beside her, his strong arms pulling his oar in exact time with hers.

She wished that she could remember being caught in those arms.

A flush come to her face at the sudden need she felt

to be held by him again, but this time when she was in full possession of her senses.

They reached the shoreline and Rupert jumped out and held the boat steady. She picked up the satchel and took his hand as she stepped out.

A tiny jolt of electricity ran through her arm at his touch and again she flushed.

She told herself firmly that she had to control such foolishness – it was only a short time ago that she had been engaged to Hamish and believed that the two of them were destined to spend the rest of their lives together.

Hamish!

She remembered now resenting the way he forced her to follow his desires rather than her own.

If Hamish wanted to go fishing and she had wanted to ride her new pony, they went fishing. If he wanted to play tennis and she thought that it would be fun to organise a croquet party, they played tennis.

If she protested at his autocratic ways, he would pull her hair, then put his arm round her shoulders and give her a hug.

It was the hug that stayed with her, not the pulling of her hair. How stupid she had been!

*

They walked over to the little cottage to retrieve the horse and trap and soon they were travelling at a fast trot to Castle Fitzalan.

"Why did you say you thought we should reach the Castle as soon as possible?" Rupert asked her.

Celina shrugged.

"I get these feelings sometimes, I always have, ever since I was a child. I don't know exactly what is going to happen, just that it will be good or bad – or *very* bad. My mother used to say it was part of my heritage as she had the same feelings and that I would grow out of them as she had. The day that she and my father were killed, I had the worst feeling ever."

Celina shuddered as she spoke, even now she could remember exactly how the black cloud had come down and engulfed her. She had screamed and screamed and no one had been unable to comfort her.

Rupert looked at her.

He did not, like so many people, seem to think that she was slightly crazy, instead he enquired gently,

"How dark was the cloud when you thought about the Castle?"

Celina repressed a sudden shiver, she could feel it all around her.

"*Dark.*"

"Then we'd better go there as quickly as possible."

Rupert cracked the whip and Jessie speeded up.

"Did you say that Lady Bruce's housekeeper had provided us with some food?"

As they drove on, Celina fed them both with hunks of bread and cheese, slices of delicious game pie and some pieces of a rich fruit cake and there was a flask of wine too.

They both ate everything heartily, although Celina could not shake off the cloud of doom that surrounded her.

She just knew for certain that something dreadful awaited them at Castle Fitzalan.

The rain Celina had foreseen now began, at first a fine mist, but soon it was deeply penetrating.

"Good Heavens, it was all bright sunshine at noon. Where did this all come from?" questioned Rupert.

"You are in the Highlands now and the weather can change in a twinkling."

By the time they reached Castle Fitzalan they were soaked through and dusk was setting in.

The big double door with its iron studs was closed.

Rupert called loudly for Duncan without any result.

Then he handed the reins to Celina, climbed down from the trap and hammered on the door, shouting for it to be opened.

Celina's sensation of disaster was by now so strong she felt sick.

Rupert came back to the trap looking very worried.

"I fear that your feelings of something being wrong are well founded. I am going round to the postern gate to see if I can get in there. Can you hold the horse and trap?"

Celina nodded, her head still throbbed horribly and she could not speak.

She watched him disappear through the rain, then she looked up at the walls. She could hear no sound from inside and her dread of what had happened here grew.

Eventually the gates in front of her creaked open.

She drove through and the gates were immediately closed behind her.

She drew the horse to a halt, then stared aghast at the sight that met her.

All over the courtyard was strewn a mess of broken furniture, pictures, papers, books, beds, pots and pans.

"*What has happened?*" she screamed.

"That is what I intend to find out," Rupert replied grimly as he helped Celina down from the trap.

As they then stood contemplating the indescribable wreckage, Celina heard a weak cry.

"It's coming from the kitchen," she gasped.

There was just enough light for them to see Duncan lying on the floor, his face a bloody mess and one of his legs sticking out at an odd angle.

Celina threw herself down beside him.

His eyes were half open and he gave another groan.

"Mistress Stirling," he moaned, "*they* came for us."

"Ssh," she soothed him. "Hush, everything will be all right now. Lord Fitzalan is here."

She looked up at Rupert, standing frustrated beside her.

"Can you find something to put some water in and a cloth so I can clean away the blood? And bring my bag from the trap, please"

Rupert ran back outside.

She had already seen that there was nothing left in the kitchen. All the utensils Duncan had used for cooking had gone, so had the table and chairs. The only piece of furniture left was the stove and blessedly a faint heat came from it and the coals were still just alight.

Celina felt Duncan's hand and took his pulse and it was rapid but strong. She felt gently round his scalp and instantly identified a nasty wound.

As her fingers explored his head, she had a sudden vivid picture of Rupert doing the same with her as she lay unconscious after falling off the staircase.

The image caused a sudden painful contraction in her breast.

Celina pushed the sensation away.

This was no time to dwell on her own feelings.

She tried to straighten his leg but Duncan cried out, his eyes opening wide and his pupils rolling up so that all she could see were the whites.

She abandoned moving his leg for the moment.

Rupert came back carrying a bowl, an old curtain, and her bag.

She took out the candles and gave them to him to light, and she filled the bowl with water from the kitchen pump and then she used the *skean dhu* to tear pieces off the curtain and started to clean the blood from Duncan's face.

"I think his leg is broken," she said. "It pains him too much for me to straighten it, but it has to be done, then it needs to be tied to a splint."

Rupert began to scout around in the kitchen and the scullery, checking what damage had been done.

Suddenly he gave a cry of triumph.

"Look what I have found!"

He appeared bearing a battered leather bottle and then found some horn drinking mugs.

"This is extremely fine whisky," he called, pouring it into one of the mugs. "Now, Duncan, this will make you feel much, much better."

He knelt on the floor, carefully lifted his retainer's head and put the mug to his lips.

"Sip this, my friend," he urged, holding the utensil until Duncan had swallowed at least half its contents.

Then he laid him back on the floor.

"I'll go and find something to make a splint and try to bring in some sort of a bed," he suggested.

Celina blessed the fact that he, Rupert, was not only intelligent but also full of resource.

While she had finished cleaning Duncan's wound, a chair leg was produced to act as a splint and then a bed was dragged in and a small pile of books found to prop it up.

The range was supplied with wood and the embers revived and the kitchen began to gather some heat.

Rupert poured out another mug of whisky.

"Now, I'm sure you'd like just a wee dram more of this, Duncan," he counselled, again kneeling and holding it to his lips.

This time when Duncan was returned to the floor, he closed his eyes and gave a gentle snore.

"Now I think it's the right time," cried out Rupert. "Thank Heavens for the Highlander's kilt!"

Celina gave a most unladylike giggle, but knew that Duncan would have hated the thought of his nether regions being exposed.

"You hold his thigh, Celina, while I straighten the lower part."

Celina gritted her teeth, drew the kilt halfway up his thigh and held it tightly.

Then she saw there was a large gash above his knee and it was bleeding.

Duncan's eyes flew open and he screeched in pain as his lower leg was pulled into its usual position and then collapsed into unconsciousness.

"Best thing that could happen," muttered Rupert, using the old curtain to bind the leg to the makeshift splint.

"There's a bullet in his thigh," exclaimed Celina, sponging the blood away. "I'll need your knife again, my Lord, to cut a bandage."

He handed her the *skean dhu*.

Without a second's hesitation she lifted up her skirt and sliced into her petticoat, tearing off a large strip to bind Duncan's wound.

"That's the very devil. I beg your pardon, Mistress Stirling. You have done a superb job, but that bullet needs to be removed. I wonder if there's a doctor around here."

Celina looked down at the unconscious Duncan.

"We need to supply him with some sort of mattress and bedclothes."

There was just enough light left to enable them to see what they were doing in the courtyard.

They then found a mattress that was almost dry and some bed clothes that had escaped the worst of the rain and together they took them into the kitchen.

"We'd better dry the wet blankets by the fire," she advised as Rupert gently lifted Duncan onto the bed.

He was so compassionate and tender, she reflected.

Here was someone who showed proper respect for a retainer. Neither her Uncle Robert nor Hamish had ever considered the feelings or wellbeing of their servants.

Rupert looked down at the injured man and then he turned.

"I must now go and see what has happened to the horses and stable Jessie. She has waited too long for her supper and I must try and find a doctor. I think Walt, the stable boy, must have run away."

Celina checked Duncan's condition and decided he was doing as well as could be expected.

She returned to the courtyard and, feeling like some kind of scavenger, sorted through the wreckage.

There were iron pots and pans that were still usable and she found a few vegetables and tins of beans. She took them inside and put a large saucepan of water on to heat.

The kitchen table was still in one piece and Celina managed to drag it into the kitchen and then she went back and found two usable chairs.

The rain had stopped, but her clothes were wet and uncomfortable and she felt thoroughly chilled.

The range was now roaring away and the kitchen was nicely warm.

Duncan however was snoring in a way that worried Celina. Could it be delayed concussion? He surely could not have had enough whisky to make him that drunk.

Moving quietly she prepared and chopped up some vegetables and managed to open a couple of tins of beans. She placed it all in one of the pans, added some hot water and put it on the stove.

Rupert came in, leading a young lad by the ear.

"This is Walt, he must have a tale to tell, if only he can be persuaded to speak."

"Where was he?"

"In the stables hiding behind a cask. Our visitors seem to have overlooked that area entirely, both Molly and Prince are fine, thank Heavens."

Celina sat down and held out her hands to the boy.

"Come and sit down, Walt."

The boy looked up at Rupert, who nodded his head and held out the second chair.

Once he was settled, Celina asked him

"Why did you not come out when we arrived?"

The lad took a deep breath and drew the back of his hand across his nose.

"I was very afeard – Mistress," he finally admitted, gulping his words. He could be no more than thirteen or so, small with hair like straw and a snub nose.

Rupert took a look at Duncan, then poured whisky into one of the horn mugs and offered it to Celina.

She shook her head and he stood leaning against the wall beside the range, sipping at his mug.

"Well, Walt, there is no need to be afraid now, so

please, tell us what happened today. You understand that we are very very upset at what has occurred here?"

Walt gulped again.

He looked from Celina to Rupert, who said nothing, as Celina smiled gently at him.

"They came – in the mornin'," he mumbled finally.

"Who came?"

It took a little time, but eventually she coaxed the story from him – and rather wished she had not.

From his description of the team of marauders, and there was no other word for them, it seemed to have been her Uncle Robert and Hamish, accompanied by several of their retainers, who had swept right into the courtyard by the postern gate.

"I forgot – to lock it," the wretched Walt confessed.

Duncan had come running out with his blunderbuss but, before he could fire, he had been first shot in the leg and then swiped with a broadsword.

He had fallen and crawled into the kitchen.

Celina, her heart nearly breaking, thought that he must have expected to die there on the floor.

Then the invaders had swarmed into the Castle.

As they had rampaged through room after room, not finding what they were seeking and frustrated beyond measure, they then threw everything they could find into the courtyard.

"They cursed a lot," said Walt. "I was hidin' in the stables, but I could see what they was – up to and I heard them shout, 'the Yankee must of found it. No doubt with that devil of our kinswoman.' That's what they said," he added nervously with a look at Celina. "Then they was off to find the Laird and you, Mistress."

She sank into the chair, the horror of the situation sweeping over her. Was there no limit to the damage her relations were willing to inflict on Lord Fitzalan?

She felt a deep sense of shame.

"Well, Walt," came in Rupert, "it was just as well you hid in the stables. Do you know where a doctor is to be found?"

Walt looked up eagerly and nodded his head.

"Aye, my Lord."

"Then you take Molly and go and fetch him. And tell the doctor that we have no idea who has inflicted these injuries on Duncan – off you go – he is depending on you."

The lad cast a look at Duncan and was gone.

Celina rose and went to the stove.

"I've tried to make a sort of vegetable stew. I don't know about you, my Lord, but I'm feeling hungry, as it's been ages since we had our picnic lunch."

"My word, so am I."

Wooden bowls were retrieved from the courtyard and rinsed out and then Celina filled them with her stew.

Rupert ate several spoonfuls before he exclaimed,

"This is food for the Gods, Mistress Stirling. You are not only a delightful companion, you cook as well!"

He continued to eat with every appearance of deep enjoyment.

Celina felt an exquisite warmth running through her body at his appreciation.

What a strange situation this was, she was thinking, looking first at the unconscious wounded retainer snoring on his bed, then at Rupert, eating her simple vegetable stew with as much joy as if it was the finest *haute cuisine*.

Then deep shame came over her as she remembered exactly what had been done to his Castle.

"I have to apologise for the way my relations have – ravaged your home," she blurted out.

"Which of us humans can choose our relations?" he answered her lightly. "We can, though, choose our friends and I hope very much that you can be mine. I am certainly yours and I have so much to thank you for – "

Celina felt tears prick at her eyes.

How could he be so generous to her?

Yet she recognised that the closeness she had felt between them on the drive from the tower had disappeared.

A thought suddenly came to her.

"What have you done with the chalice, my Lord?"

He smiled at her.

"I have hidden it in the stable bran tub, still inside the satchel. Tomorrow morning I must search through all that debris to see if I can find the book with the family tree. We must discover exactly how the inheritance goes from generation to generation."

Celina nodded.

Until that line was firmly established, the feud over the ownership of the chalice would continue. She was very much afraid however that it belonged to her Uncle Robert.

Which was yet another reason as to why any sort of relationship between her and Rupert must be doomed.

"Now I must find you a bed for the night," he said. "By rights you should be restored to Lady Bruce, but I just cannot see how that can be achieved."

Celina shook her head.

"I would not like to leave Duncan until a doctor has seen him."

A further search of the courtyard produced another bed. Rupert dragged it into a reception room, then found a reasonably dry mattress, bed linen and feather coverlet.

He lit a fire in the salon, set all the bedding around it to warm, then once more went back to the courtyard.

He came into the kitchen with an armful of clothes.

"They threw a whole wardrobe down and look what it contained!"

He spread out a selection of garments. They were old fashioned and smelled of mothballs but they were dry.

"I think these clothes belonged to my grandmother, but I hope you may be able to make use of them. Alas, my luggage has been scattered and all my clothes are ruined. However, I have found this old kilt – it must have been my grandfather's."

She recognised the Fitzalan tartan.

"And it's dry too?" she asked.

"It is and it was in a chest with some other useful items. We can both change out of our damp clothes."

Celina was overjoyed.

She chose the first gown that came to hand from the pile and some undergarments, then retired to the reception room.

When she returned to the kitchen, enjoying feeling dry at last, Rupert looked startled.

"Forgive me but you look so like my grandmother," he cried. "Her hair was not your gorgeous red, but in the portrait that hangs upstairs, at least it used to hang upstairs, but I am afraid it is one of the casualties in the courtyard now, she wears a dress so very like that one and she carries herself as you do."

Celina had given no thought as to the attractiveness of the garments she had chosen. Now she looked down at the green velvet of her gown and was grateful that she had chosen it.

"What do you think of my outfit?" Rupert asked, striking a pose.

Celina was stunned at his appearance.

He looked almost unrecognisable. Gone was the sophisticated American in his three-piece suit.

In his place stood a Highland Clan Chief in kilt and velvet jacket worn with a linen shirt. His shoulders were not as broad as those of Hamish, but his legs were every bit as good – strong and muscular.

"Welcome, Lord Fitzalan," she smiled. "You have entered into your Highland heritage!"

He gave a sheepish smile.

"I have been wondering if I should acquire a kilt, but I was afraid I might let my grandfather's ghost down if I don't have the knees!"

"You have the knees," she assured him gravely.

They stood for a moment gazing at each other.

Then there was a knock on the door and the doctor entered.

He accepted the chaos all around him remarkably calmly and he questioned them closely about the treatment they had given Duncan and then he inspected the patient.

Finally he spoke up,

"I compliment you, Miss Stirling, on the way you have dealt with matters. Duncan, here, is fortunate to have had your services. Now, I will remove the bullet from his thigh. You have hot water? Excellent. Be so good as to attend me please."

The bullet was efficiently removed.

Then the wound was cleaned and bound up with a bandage the doctor produced from his case.

At the end of the procedure, he enquired,

"You have no idea who it was who inflicted these horrendous injuries?"

Rupert shook his head.

"Unfortunately not."

The doctor gave him an old fashioned look.

"I hope that we are not returning to the old days of feuds between the Clans!"

"I have recently returned from America to claim my inheritance. I know nothing about Clan feuds."

"I see."

The doctor eyed his kilt.

"Well, as to your patient, try to get him to drink some water and keep him warm. I'll call again tomorrow and hope by then that he will have regained consciousness. I commend your nursing skills, Miss Stirling."

After the doctor left, Rupert insisted Celina retire.

"I will be with Duncan in case he needs anything."

Celina cleaned her face and her teeth as well as she could by the pump and retired to her makeshift bed.

She lay there hypnotised by the flickering shadows the fire threw on the walls and ceiling.

Her last thought before slipping into sleep was that the MacLeans had destroyed any chance of happiness for her in the future.

CHAPTER NINE

As Celina prepared for the night, Rupert went back into the rubbish-strewn courtyard.

He stood still for a moment hands on hips thinking about the beautiful girl who had been by his side for what now seemed like weeks rather than days.

Now that they had found the heirloom, would she vanish from his life?

He sensed her withdrawal from him the moment it was confirmed that it was the MacLeans who had wrecked the interior of Castle Fitzalan.

He wondered why they had not set fire to the place, but perhaps burning down a castle was too difficult a task.

He had to find some way to convince Celina that, as far as he was concerned, her relationship to those dastardly marauders did not matter a jot.

She definitely came from a different mould.

Her honesty, clear-sightedness and high principles removed her from any comparison with Lord MacLean and his son – they were no better than common criminals.

In the gold fields of California, Rupert had found men who took what they wanted with little mercy and no regard for the law. He had not expected to find the same attitude in Scotland.

The weather had cleared again and now an almost full moon lit the desolation around him with painful clarity.

How, he only wondered, could a wonderful girl like

Celina possibly be related to the thugs who had performed this desecration?

The possibility that the MacLeans might prove to be the owners of the ancient chalice was deeply unsettling.

He urgently needed to find the book with the family tree – it had to be somewhere here among the litter in the courtyard for only the odd pieces of paper remained in the muniment room.

Rupert started pulling pieces of furniture upright, assessing how much damage was done. He soon gave up, as most of the items were only fit for firewood.

For the first time he now applauded the way that his grandfather had sold off anything of value.

The books all seemed to have been carted out and dumped into a pile, and ashes suggested the MacLeans had tried to set fire to them. Perhaps the rain had made that too difficult a task.

Rupert picked up several sodden books, then found some that had been shielded from the wet.

He carried as many as he could inside, all the time checking for the one with the family tree.

Finally he arranged a makeshift bed for himself in the kitchen and collapsed onto it in exhaustion.

*

Several times during the night a groan or loud snore from Duncan woke Rupert.

Each time he would light a candle and check on the injured man.

Each time before he went back to his bed, he would look longingly in the direction of the salon where Celina was asleep and stifle a temptation to steal in and see if she needed anything.

He could not help imagining her glorious red hair spread over her pillow, her lovely face relaxed in sleep.

He woke for a final time at dawn and Duncan at last seemed to be sleeping peacefully.

Rupert riddled the range, added coal, put water on, then dressed in his now dry suit and went to look for some coffee.

He gave out a whoop of joy when he found not only some beans but also the coffee grinder.

He made himself a mug and settled down to scan the pile he had made of the most promising-looking books.

Fitzalan, MacLean, Beaumarche – how did all these names fit together?

He needed that family tree.

Only one book proved of any interest.

Claiming to be a history of the Fitzalan family, it proved to be little more than a collection of anecdotes.

A skim through the book produced only one brief mention of a lost and unidentified treasure, but there was no family tree.

He went out again to search for more books feeling thoroughly frustrated.

Until ownership of the chalice was established this damaging and stupid feud could not be ended.

Returning to the kitchen with an armful of yet more possible books, he found Celina dressed in her own clothes and wearing her hair in a long plait over one shoulder.

"See," she said delightedly. "Duncan has regained consciousness."

A thrill of relief ran through Rupert.

Duncan was sitting up in bed. He looked very pale but his eyes were bright.

"What's the Laird been up to, eh?" he gurgled.

Rupert showed them both the collection of books.

"I'm looking for a family tree. I've been trying to find the book I glimpsed when we were searching through the muniment room the other day."

He looked at Celina stirring a pot on the range.

"What are you cooking?"

"Porridge – it's the best Scottish breakfast there is. Tradition says it should be cooked in a drawer overnight, but we'll have to forget that."

Duncan gave another little chuckle, he seemed to be coming back to life and getting stronger every minute.

"She's a wee bonnie lass all right, but can she cook porridge? That's the true test of a Scottish cook!"

He looked at the books Rupert put on the table.

"Could you no find the Bible, laddie?"

"The Bible? The family tree I saw was not in the Good Book."

"Mebbe not, but a list of the family is."

Celina held out a bowl of porridge.

"Could you please take this out to Walt before you start searching the courtyard again?"

The events of the previous day had badly upset the boy and Rupert took time to reassure him that everything would be all right before starting his search for the Bible.

As he turned over the debris, he realised how much he would miss both Duncan and Walt when the time came to return to New York.

As for Celina –

For the moment he pushed all thought of her aside.

He soon found an old and heavy tome. The leather

binding had suffered badly from the rain, but the contents seemed to have survived.

He took it back inside.

Celina handed him a bowl of porridge.

"Research can wait until you have eaten breakfast," she insisted with a smile, "and I've made coffee."

"The porridge'll be best with a wee dram of whisky round the edge," added Duncan with a sly smile.

Rupert reached out for the bottle he had found the night before.

"There may just be enough," he laughed, pouring it into the bowl.

He sat down and fed Duncan the warming porridge.

"She's as bonnie a cook as she looks," Duncan said after a few mouthfuls. "But I think I'll sleep for a wee bit."

He closed his eyes and slumped down onto the bed. Rupert helped to make his splinted leg more comfortable and then studied him with worried eyes.

"He is breathing quite easily," commented Celina, joining him at the bedside. "I think he just needs sleep."

She sat down at the table and opened the Bible.

Rupert picked up his bowl of porridge, it was warm and filling but for him it could not replace eggs and hash brown potatoes.

"It's a little difficult to work out the details," Celina remarked, looking up from the Bible. "It starts in the early seventeenth century, but an effort has been made to fill in some of the past. Lots of different hands make the later entries and I need to try and draw up a proper family tree."

Rupert returned to the muniment room and picked up the odd pieces of paper littering the floor.

Several were only written on one side and he took

them into the kitchen and gave them all to Celina together with a propelling pencil from his jacket pocket.

He sat in the other chair and enjoyed studying her serious face as she concentrated on working out the details for the family tree from the information in the Bible.

She was, he decided, the most beautiful girl he had ever seen.

Suddenly she looked up at him, flushed as she met his gaze and hastily looked back at her work.

"I think I have been able to decipher some sort of a tree."

She pushed two pieces of paper across the table.

She came and stood at his shoulder, using his pencil to point out the relevant entries.

"As you see here, the family was originally called Beaumarche and a Frenchman probably married a Scottish heiress at some stage. The 1745 rising when Bonnie Prince Charlie tried to gain the English throne, proved disastrous for the Beaumarches, as for so many Scottish families.

"Two of the young male offspring survived. One died without issue at the age of twenty-four – that's him."

The pencil pointed.

"His brother had two daughters and was the last of the male Beaumarches."

Celina indicated two more entries.

"The elder daughter married a cousin of hers who was granted the title of Lord Fitzalan, the younger one Lord MacLean."

She looked up at him.

"Do you realise that means you are distantly related not only to me, but also to my uncle, Lord MacLean, and to Hamish MacLean?"

Rupert felt a thrill at any connection with Celina, however remote, but a relationship with the MacLeans was a different matter.

He looked across the table with a grim smile.

"I cannot think your uncle and cousin will greet the news that I am a long-lost cousin of theirs with delight!"

Celina's pencil still hovered over the family tree.

"The fact that you are the Lord Fitzalan proves that your line is the more senior, but does not explain why the MacLeans possess Beaumarche Castle."

Rupert reached for the history of his family.

"Maybe there is something in here that will tell us."

Celina made more coffee and checked on Duncan.

"He's still asleep and seems to be fine."

Rupert looked up in triumph.

"It's all here in this book! Apparently the last male Beaumarche left two great Scottish estates – Beaumarche and Fitzalan – each with an imposing Castle. His will said that each daughter should inherit a Castle, but did not say which each should have.

"Beaumarche was deemed the most beautiful Castle and was where the family lived. The elder daughter said it should be hers while the younger said Castle Fitzalan was the older dwelling and should therefore go to the elder girl.

"After arguing bitterly, they finally agreed to throw dice. The younger sister won in the end and then claimed Beaumarche. They never spoke to each other again."

Rupert closed the book and looked at Celina.

"So that is why the MacLeans possess Beaumarche and that is when the feuding began. Neither husband was apparently very satisfactory and the book says the division of the estates began a decline in the family fortunes."

"How sad," sighed Celina, pouring out fresh coffee. "All that bad blood. You don't seem to have inherited any of it, though."

"Nor do you," added Rupert, looking at Celina and thinking how exquisite she looked, standing by the range, her flaming hair dressed in a long plait, the faint powdering of freckles giving her skin a golden glow.

For a long moment they looked at each other and Rupert felt his pulse beating faster and faster.

Celina's golden glow deepened to a rosy flush.

Hardly knowing what he was doing, Rupert rose –

And at that moment the doctor came bustling in.

"Morning, Lord Fitzalan, Miss Stirling," he nodded to them both. "I have come to see how my patient fares."

Grateful though Rupert was to see him, he wished the doctor could have delayed his arrival.

Duncan woke up and after an inspection, the doctor pronounced him,

"A stout fellow with a constitution of iron. In time you should do splendidly, but there will be a limp for the rest of your life."

"Och, weel, so long as I have me leg, that will be no trouble," blustered Duncan.

The doctor laughed, returned his stethoscope to his case and said he would drop by and plaster the leg the next day.

Rupert accompanied him outside.

"You have a dickens of a task here, my Lord," the doctor commented, looking at the chaos in the courtyard.

Rupert grunted and said nothing.

"But I have no doubt you will tackle it with great Fitzalan spirit. Your grandfather was a feisty man and so was your father and it was such a sad day when he left for America – and a happy one that has seen your return.

"Your man, Duncan, should pull through, but watch for a relapse. I don't like what you told me of his condition during the night. It sounds like a late-onset concussion and he is hardly in the prime of life and Miss Stirling seems a sensible nurse."

Rupert was suddenly aware that Celina staying with him without a chaperone would not look very good.

"She should be with Lady Bruce. It is unfortunate that the bad weather and Duncan's condition, together with what has happened here," he waved a hand at the courtyard debris, "meant she could not go to Drumlanrigg last night."

"Don't you worry at all, my Lord. There'll be no spreading of the fact from me, I assure you. I'll be off. If you're worried about your man's condition, send that lad for me."

Rupert assisted the doctor into his trap and closed the gates behind him.

Then he rescued the satchel with the chalice from the stable bran bin and instructed Walt to saddle Prince and find his saddlebags.

Returning inside, Rupert took Celina into the salon and told her what the doctor had said.

Then he gave her a straight look.

"I am going over to Beaumarche Castle to prove to Lord MacLean and Hamish that they have no claim on the chalice and that this feud must end here."

For a moment Celina stood rigid.

"I will come with you, my Lord. I am the only one who might be able to make Uncle Robert see sense."

Rupert placed a hand on Celina's shoulder.

He could feel the tension in her body.

Was she afraid for him?

"Duncan needs you to look after him, Celina. Walt cannot do it. I am sure that when Lord MacLean sees the documents, he will have to accept the situation."

Celina closed her eyes and swayed slightly.

Then she looked straight at him.

"I must come with you. You need me there."

Rupert wanted to say he needed her at his side for ever, but he knew that until this stupid feud was brought to an end, his feelings for Celina must remain unspoken.

He resisted the urge to take her in his arms.

"I do appreciate your concern for me and for your uncle and cousin and I will come straight back and tell you what has happened."

She looked desperately at him.

"You know what the MacLeans are like. At least take a gun with you."

Rupert shook his head.

"That would bring myself down to their level. This has to be a completely rational discussion."

Celina let out a cry of frustration.

"Can't you understand my Uncle Robert does not understand the meaning of 'rational discussion'. He only understands the rule of force and the importance of being stronger than your enemy."

"I shall prove that I am not his enemy."

"But to him you are!" Celina screamed at him.

Tears ran down her cheeks.

Rupert looked at her and would have taken her in his arms but Walt entered.

"I've harnessed Prince and here're the saddlebags."

Celina picked up her drawstring bag.

Rupert thanked Walt and said he would be out in a moment.

"Then you must take this with you," Celina insisted fiercely, holding out a revolver.

He looked at it in astonishment.

"Have you had that with you all this time?"

"I took it from Uncle Robert's gun room before I helped you to escape from Beaumarche. I kept it because when I saw what he and Hamish were capable of, I wanted to be able to defend myself."

"Then you must keep it with you now," said Rupert softly, "and make sure the old blunderbuss is loaded. You can teach Walt how to use it."

She dashed away her tears with an angry hand.

"*Please*, please take it."

He shook his head, went through to the kitchen and placed the satchel into a saddlebag, together with the Bible, the family tree that Celina had drawn up and the Fitzalan family history.

Duncan watched him.

"Ye're off to sort out the MacLeans, laddie?"

Rupert nodded.

"You look after things here, Duncan."

Celina appeared in the doorway, her expression was hopeless.

Rupert found that he was too choked with emotion to say anything to her.

He raised a hand in farewell and turned to go.

Suddenly she rushed over the room, flung her arms around him and buried her head in his chest.

"You *must* come back," she cried at him. "Promise me you'll come back!"

He dropped the saddlebags and crushed her in his arms for an instant, then let her go, picked up the bags and left.

*

The sun shone brightly and Prince appeared to be delighted to have his Master on his back and happily ate up the miles between the two estates.

At Beaumarche Castle, a groom came out from the stables and held Prince as Rupert dismounted and took the saddlebags over his arm.

He told the man he would not be long, and strode towards the house.

Lord MacLean emerged with Hamish behind him.

"You are not at all welcome here," growled Lord MacLean at him arrogantly, but his eyes shifted uneasily and Rupert knew that his appearance had unsettled him.

"You have brought such devastating damage to my home and failed to find the Beaumarche heirloom," Rupert said coldly. "I have come to tell you the truth of the matter before you are arrested for the sacking of Castle Fitzalan. Law Officers are on their way."

Hamish cracked an uncertain laugh.

"Law Officers! You have no proof we have done anything."

"I have witnesses – " Rupert responded steadily.

"The dead cannot witness," snarled Hamish, his lip curling disdainfully.

"Be silent!" his father commanded.

"Your words should be enough to condemn you. However, you are making a habit of leaving your victims for dead without ensuring that they actually are. Duncan's head is far too solid for him to be despatched by a blow from you, and you failed to find a terrified stable lad. Both saw you and can identify you."

Lord MacLean and Hamish exchanged looks, then turned and retreated inside, slamming the door in Rupert's face.

He forced it open and followed them into the Great Hall.

Lord MacLean flung himself into a chair, drew one of the bottles that littered the table towards him, filled a glass with whisky and took a deep draught.

"You claim to know the truth about the heirloom," he snarled without looking at Rupert. "*What* is this truth?"

Rupert placed his saddlebags on the table.

Hamish sat down on his father's right, lolling in an insulting manner and supplied himself with whisky.

"Brought it with you?" he asked in a taunting voice. "Going to give it to us?"

He produced a revolver from his waist and pointed it at Rupert.

Rupert refused to be daunted.

Opening the saddlebags, he produced his pieces of evidence.

"So you see," he asserted, pointing to the relevant entries in the Bible and Celina's family tree, "extraordinary as it seems, we are remote cousins."

Lord MacLean and Hamish seemed quite incapable of registering this fact. Their attention was riveted on the satchel which Rupert produced last of all.

"*This* is the Beaumarche heirloom," he announced.

To silence he unwrapped and placed the chalice on the table.

Amidst such a collection of empty and half-empty bottles, the golden chalice glowed with an unearthly light.

For a moment the two MacLeans were transfixed.

"Then the Beaumarche heirloom," Lord MacLean crowed triumphantly, "you admit it is *ours*!"

He grabbed the chalice and held it up, turning it this way and that.

"No," Rupert asserted firmly. "*It is not.*"

He produced the document stating that the chalice was the inheritance of the eldest Beaumarche son and went back over the family tree again.

"So as the Beaumarche male line ran out in 1793, the chalice is vested in the Crown."

"*No!*" roared Lord MacLean.

With his free hand he swept the books and papers off the table.

He looked expectantly at Hamish.

"*Shoot him!*"

CHAPTER TEN

Celina remained in the kitchen and listened to the sound of the horse's hooves vanishing into the distance.

"Ye love the laddie," Duncan grunted, opening his eyes.

Desolation gripped Celina.

She was certain she would never see Rupert alive again.

"And it's that plain he's stricken with ye," added Duncan happily.

Celina hardly heard him.

She felt deeply that her uncle would never allow his enemy to walk away free from Beaumarche and she knew Rupert had taken hold of her heart in a way that Hamish had never come near to achieving.

The revelation that had shown her the dark side of the MacLeans had also brought her true love.

She had never felt for Hamish the passion that now consumed her for Rupert.

He was her perfect gentle knight – a man not only handsome and strong with all the physical attributes that she had once admired in Hamish, but had characteristics he lacked.

This was a man of deep principles, intelligence and compassion.

He made her laugh, had opened her eyes to a life beyond Scotland and shown her consideration and respect.

And now he intended to put himself at the mercy of

her uncle – a man who knew no mercy, a man possessed of a primitive urge to take whatever he wanted at any time.

Which would include the Beaumarche heirloom.

"The Laird'll be alright," Duncan now assured her. "He's a man who can take care of himsel."

She tried to feel as confident as he was.

"Is it that you want to follow him, lassie? Ye ken fine well ye can leave me. I need no nursin' now."

He tried to put his wounded leg on the ground and strangled a cry of pain.

She rushed over to prevent him from putting any of his weight on the leg.

"Not until it's in plaster, Duncan. After the doctor has done that, then you can try standing."

He allowed her to return his leg to the bed.

"I see I canna stand for now, but that dinna mean I need ye here, lassie."

Celina looked at brave Duncan, trying to appear full of life and able to take care of himself. She just could not abandon a man who had undergone such punishment – and at the hands of her own relatives.

"Duncan, of course you are fine now, but my place is here. Lord Fitzalan would be very upset if he discovered that I had left you."

She went out into the courtyard to hide her tears.

There Walt brought her three eggs and a couple of carrots from the Castle's small garden.

"We may be able to eat after all," she said, smiling at him.

Then she remembered what Rupert had said to her about teaching the boy how to handle the blunderbuss.

Here was a task for Duncan.

Leaving him instructing Walt, Celina went back out to the courtyard with some idea of trying to find an activity that would banish her vision of Rupert walking into a trap at Beaumarche Castle.

There came a pounding at the gate.

Opening it she found a horse carrying two people she immediately recognised.

"Her Ladyship has sent us," piped up Gordon Hall, Lady Bruce's Steward, leading in his horse and helping the maid who had been looking after Celina at Lady Bruce's down from her pillion seat.

"When you didna return last night, she was afeard things had not gone right. If I found all in order here, I was to leave Mary with you and return to Drumlanrigg."

Celina clearly understood the unspoken message – Lady Bruce was worried for her reputation.

She hoped that sending Mary to her would at least give her a semblance of propriety.

Celina turned to Gordon.

"I have to go after Lord Fitzalan," she explained. "Lord MacLean – "

The Steward knew only too well exactly what her uncle was capable of.

"If you and Mary are here to watch over Duncan, then I can leave."

She called Walt and told him to harness the fastest of the horses in the Fitzalan stable.

He looked abashed.

"There isna one here that's fast, miss. Jessie's the strongest, she's the one that pulled the trap."

"Then harness Jessie, and please be as quick as you can, Walt."

"And we havena a side saddle."

"An ordinary one will be fine."

He ran off.

The two servants looked aghast at the state of the courtyard.

Mary clutched a bundle and she handed it to Celina.

"It's a change of clothes, miss," she said, giving a little dip of a curtsy.

Celina took the bundle gratefully.

While Walt was harnessing Jessie, she went into the salon and put on the fresh clothes, relieved to see that the skirt was a full one.

Then she carefully loaded the revolver, ensured the safety catch was on and stuck it into her waistband.

Walt brought her the little mare that had done such splendid work pulling the trap.

Celina inspected the saddle and recalled the days when she first went to live with the MacLeans and always rode astride, until Lady Bruce insisted that she was too old for such ragamuffin ways and must ride side saddle.

"Help me up, please," she asked the Steward.

"Her Ladyship will no be pleased to hear ye're to ride like that, Mistress Stirling," he objected.

"Maybe she will not have to hear," replied Celina, adjusting her skirt to accommodate her legs astride.

She settled her revolver more comfortably and then dug her heels into Jessie's side.

A few moments later she was out of the Castle and heading towards Beaumarche.

She soon recognised that Walt had been right about Jessie's speed.

Celina reckoned that Rupert on Prince would travel

much faster than she could. However, he did not have her familiarity with the countryside.

There was a way over rough land that shortened the distance between the Castles Fitzalan and Beaumarche. It involved negotiating a narrow ledge round the side of the mountain that reared up between the two estates.

As long as Jessie was not scared of the straight fall to the river below, then the route would mean she should reach Beaumarche not too far behind Rupert.

Celina's heart was in her mouth as they reached the narrow and precipitous path.

The horse might not be speedy, but she was brave and trusting. Jessie did not flinch for a moment and after ten minutes of heart-stopping balancing, the path widened and soon they were trotting along in perfect safety.

The towers of Beaumarche Castle came into view.

As though the horse realised what was needed, she put on a spurt and very soon they were clopping over the cobbles of the stable yard.

She dismounted before a groom emerged.

His eyes widened as he saw her.

"Hello, Tam," Celina called out as though nothing could be more natural than that she should ride in astride a strange horse.

"Lord MacLean and Hamish at home, are they?"

Tam gulped.

"Aye, Mistress Celina, that they are. And they've a visitor with them."

"Ah, that'll be Lord Fitzalan," remarked Celina in a conversational tone. "I'm glad to have caught him. Been here long?"

Tam shook his head nonplussed.

"Not long at all."

The perilous journey over the mountain had gained her valuable time.

"Look after Jessie for me, will you? She could do with a drink, a rub-down and some oats."

She tossed him the reins and walked calmly off into the house.

Using the back entrance, she stole past the kitchen without being noticed, took off her shoes and in stockinged feet crept noiselessly along to the service side of the Great Hall screen.

Through its carving, she could see Lord MacLean and Hamish sitting at the refectory table and facing them was Rupert.

Celina felt her heart contract as she heard his voice, measured and calm, relating to them the facts regarding the inheritance of the chalice.

Then she saw that her uncle held it in his grasp.

She could imagine the light of possession that must be sparkling in his eyes.

There came a sudden roar,

"*No!*"

Books and documents were swept onto the floor.

Then,

"*Shoot him!*"

Celina had not realised until then that Hamish held a gun. She caught her breath and cursed the fact she had not drawn her revolver and removed the safety catch.

There was no chance she could fire before Hamish.

But she could shoot him afterwards.

She pulled out the revolver.

"No, Father," now murmured Hamish. "Were you not listening? That chalice does not belong to us. The old Laird was right all along. We have no title to it."

"Hamish, we inherited the Beaumarche estate, it's *ours*. Shoot the blackguard and then there will be none to argue otherwise."

Celina's heart beat frantically.

Should she shoot or wait to see if Hamish won out over his father for the first time in his life?

Hamish stood up straight.

"You stupid old man! You're ruining all our lives. You lost me the woman I love – and now you want me to commit murder."

Lord MacLean sat very still.

Celina could well imagine his eyes narrowing as he regarded his son and heir.

"What foolishness is this, boy?"

His voice was steely quiet.

"You were eager enough to attack this upstart, this apology for a Highland Laird, before. What has changed?"

"Maybe I have," Hamish sounded tired. "Maybe I no longer want to carry on with this useless feud."

"But without this," Lord MacLean now held up the golden chalice, "we will lose Beaumarche. With it we can clear our debts and start again."

Rupert intervened.

"I am willing to lend you money – if it will end this horror."

"A Fitzalan varlet to lend us money?" roared Lord MacLean. "So you can have us in a vice? Never! Shoot, Hamish, shoot him!"

Celina then moved silently into the Great Hall and aimed her revolver at Hamish.

None of the men saw her.

Before she could fire, Hamish threw his gun on the table and stated firmly,

"No, Father. It's over!"

Lord MacLean picked up the weapon.

"Then, by God, *I will*."

Before he could shoot, Celina pulled her trigger.

Lord MacLean collapsed in his chair.

"Father!" cried Hamish, bending over him.

Celina came forward.

She was shaking.

Lord MacLean looked at her, his eyes full of hatred.

"You have betrayed us, your own kin," he hissed, his voice was low and heavy with passion, as his left hand grasped his wounded shoulder.

The gun he had been holding dropped to the floor.

Rupert kicked it to the back of the Great Hall, out of reach of both Hamish and his father, and then picked up the chalice from where it had fallen onto the table.

"Uncle Robert, I loved you once," Celina spoke up, forcing her voice to be steady. "Both you and Hamish."

She looked across at the young man standing on the other side of the table, his face pale and agonised.

"You have destroyed that love. I cannot deny my MacLean heritage, but all my loyalty is now given to the Fitzalans. I am sure Lord Fitzalan has explained that we are all distant relations."

She saw Rupert raise a hand towards her – and then drop it again.

"If you continue to perpetuate this horrible feud, I shall stand beside your enemy."

She then moved towards Rupert.

A shiver ran through Lord MacLean and he seemed to shrink in his chair.

He looked at Hamish.

"Help me, son," he stammered in a voice that had lost all its usual authority. "I bleed."

As if he had suddenly awoken from a deep coma, Hamish bellowed for a servant, grabbed a napkin from off the table, ripped the torn sleeve from his father's wounded shoulder, poured whisky over it then held the napkin firmly against the bullet wound.

As a servant came running, he ordered clean water and bandages.

Celina had seen Hamish act with the same skill and speed on the hunting field.

She then collapsed into a chair, placed her revolver on the table and hugged herself to try and stop shaking.

Rupert poured whisky into a horn cup and handed it to her.

"Once again, Mistress Stirling, you have saved my life."

There was something in his voice that seemed to open a chasm between them and a chill entered her heart.

"When can we expect the Law Officers to arrive?" enquired Hamish.

"Ah," responded Rupert. "I did not actually have time to alert them before my arrival."

Hamish stared at him in silence for a while.

"Will you be summoning them after you leave?"

"That all depends on you and your father, Hamish MacLean. Swear to end this ridiculous feud now and I will then ignore everything that has happened since my arrival in Scotland. If not, I will lay my evidence before the Law and have you and your father here arrested on a charge of breaking and entering, not to mention assault and battery."

Hamish looked at his father and back at Rupert.

"*I give you my word that the feud ends now.*"

"And you, Lord MacLean?"

Hate filled the eyes that glared back at Rupert, but Celina could see that all his spirit and energy had seeped away. He, who had always looked so much younger than his years, now looked even older than he was.

Slowly he nodded his head and mumbled,

"Aye, you have the word of a MacLean – "

"Then that is good enough for me."

Hamish looked across at Celina and pleaded,

"Will you not return to me, Celina? You know my heart is yours."

She shook her head.

"What we had is over, Hamish."

She drained the last of the whisky, rose and started to gather up the books and documents from the floor.

Rupert picked up the chalice.

"The Beaumarche heirloom will be handed to the Crown," he stated. "I hope that it can be displayed so that all may see and appreciate its sublime beauty. It has been hidden away for long enough."

He looked across at Hamish.

"Please will you consider the offer I made of a loan. The fact that we are very distantly related should make it possible for you to accept and it would be no more than a commercial transaction to enable the MacLean estate to put itself onto a sound footing."

Hamish said nothing and Celina took this to mean that later he would accept Rupert's offer.

Rupert wrapped up the chalice in the piece of plaid that had protected it for so many centuries and returned it to the satchel.

Celina added all the books and documents and then she turned to Rupert,

"Will you escort me to Drumlanrigg, my Lord?"

He held out his arm.

"It will be my honour, Mistress Stirling!"

Celina could feel Hamish's gaze burning into her back as they walked slowly away.

She hoped never again to enter the Great Hall of Beaumarche Castle.

*

They retrieved their mounts and Rupert smiled as he helped Celina onto Jessie.

She tried to pull her skirts over her stockinged legs without much success.

"I'll not have you laughing at poor Jessie now," she admonished him. "Not when she has done so much."

Immediately his expression sobered.

"And you will please remember that the sight of my lower limbs is unmentionable in polite society," she added.

"The least I can do to thank you as well as Jessie for having saved my life is to forget that I have ever seen your lower limbs!" he answered her with solemnity as they rode out of the stable yard.

"I left Duncan in good hands with Gordon Hall and Mary," she told him.

"I felt certain you would not have left him alone. I'm glad to hear he is in good hands and that I can return you to Drumlanrigg now. Then I must arrange for proper supplies for Castle Fitzalan."

Celina could hardly bear it that he had said nothing affectionate to her.

Her heart seemed to be breaking inside her breast.

"Lady Bruce must have been rather worried about your reputation – "

His voice sounded constricted.

"She knows that I am sensible enough for her not to need to worry about such things," she replied awkwardly.

What should she do if he felt that he ought to offer her marriage to save her reputation?

Even though it was her dearest desire, she could not accept him for such a reason.

He glanced across at her, but said nothing.

They left Beaumarche behind, climbing up into the moorland that led over the hills towards Drumlanrigg.

"Will you hand over the chalice in person? I shall not feel happy until it has been safely bestowed," Celina remarked after a little, hating the silence between them.

"Yes, it is far too precious to be entrusted to anyone else, but would you anticipate your relations going back on their word?"

"No!" she asserted at once. "The MacLean honour will not allow them to break a solemn word."

"I am pleased to hear you say so."

Rupert suddenly reined in and Celina then brought Jessie to a halt, wondering why they needed to stop.

He looked around them and she followed his gaze.

The sun was shining brightly and the mountains in the distance held a blue haze.

Far away could be seen the sparkle of a small loch.

There was a stream running through the moors, its brown water gurgling musically over bright stones.

High above them a lark sang in the clear air.

Celina mused that she should be feeling at one with this lovely scene, but inside it seemed as though her life's blood was slowly seeping away.

Then Rupert dismounted and came to her side.

"Mistress Stirling – will you get down for a while?" he murmured, his words jerky.

For a few moments they stood in silence while their horses nuzzled each other.

Rupert drew in a deep breath.

"This air – it's like no other I've known. So clear, so pure, so life enhancing, so like this wonderful scenery."

He turned to look at Celina.

"Without you, my extremely dear Mistress Stirling, I would *not* be here to enjoy all of this."

She started to protest, but he stopped her at once with a raised hand.

"No, please let me finish. From the start of my stay in Scotland you have rescued me, supported me and today saved my life again. In return you have had your own life turned upside down and lost your respect for the relations who have loved and raised you. I can *never* repay the debt I owe you."

Celina felt dark depression settle on her.

He did not love her, but was going to offer marriage to try and repay that debt.

She knew she could never accept such a proposal.

He took her hand, folded her slight fingers around his, brought them to his lips and continued,

"This terrible feud that has just ended threatened to destroy any chance I may have of future happiness – "

A shiver ran through Celina.

"It has prevented me from giving you the trust you deserved and prevented me acknowledging that, right from my first sight of you in that Great Hall, I had fallen in love with the most beautiful girl I have ever seen."

She raised her eyes to his, not quite able to believe the words she was hearing.

His eyes looked deep into hers.

"A girl who is so much more than beautiful. One who is intelligent, strong, compassionate, honourable – one who lives by the principles I try to follow in my own life."

Celina almost smiled.

He was now saying exactly what she had thought that very morning about him!

"The fact is that I am so deep in debt to you, I fear means you may not take my words for what they are, that you may think I feel I am in honour bound to make you an offer of marriage.

"Oh, my darling girl, can I make you believe that you are my heart's delight? That without you by my side, life will always be cold and drab?

"That you have revealed to me beyond my wildest imagination that love can and does conquer all now and for evermore.

"That I do not care if you cannot face dividing a life between Scotland and America.

"That I will willingly move permanently to Castle Fitzalan if only you will say you will be my wife."

The lark was still singing in the sky and now Celina could feel its blissful song filling every vein in her body with such happiness she thought she would die.

The eyes that looked into hers were filled with so much love, she knew without any doubt that he felt exactly as she did.

"My darling Rupert," she murmured, pressing the hand that held hers. "If you didn't love me, if we could not share our life together – and I care not where it be lived – then I would shrivel and wither.

"I adore you, my Lord Fitzalan, from the top to the very bottom of my soul – "

He took her in his arms, drew her close to his breast and kissed her.

Celina felt glorious sunshine burst around her in an explosion of light.

It was as though he had taken her up to Heaven.

She clasped her arms tightly around his neck and felt her body dissolve into his.

THE REVELATION IS LOVE

"A bowl of one of your soups a little later, Duncan, would be great, but I think Miss Stirling and I should start our search right away."

Rupert looked at Celina.

"Should we start at the top or the bottom?"

"The top," suggested Celina briskly.

She was feeling uncomfortable at the closeness of this man and the light in his eyes as he looked at her.

Not even Hamish had stirred such a complex set of emotions in her.

If only he was not a Fitzalan!

THE BARBARA CARTLAND PINK COLLECTION

Titles in this series